I Can Hear Everything from Here

Short Stories

Mark Walling

I Can Hear Everything from Here

Cover Image: *April, Oklahoma* by Steven Schroeder
Book Design: Rowan Kehn

ISBN: 979-8-9868994-1-1

Turning Plow Press

For Bethany

Contents

The Year I Lost My Ass

This was the year I lost my ass.

I'm not talking financials.

I took it as a sign I was dying. That I had a terminal disease.

My wife said it looked like I'd taken a dump in my pants. She didn't laugh until she saw I wasn't. It became her favorite phrase.

This was the year I tore down the playhouse in the backyard. My wife said the removal of the playhouse would open up the space. Let it breathe. Our daughter doesn't like to play in it by herself and is too young to have an opinion about the yard. She breathes fine but she cries a lot and often doesn't sleep well.

We didn't have the money to pay someone. The remodeling of our house was supposed to take six weeks. We stopped counting at thirty. I said we didn't buy a new house because it was gonna cost too much and be too much trouble. Remember? I didn't laugh until I saw my wife wasn't. It became my favorite phrase.

I told my wife I would tear down the playhouse. I told her it would take a month.

This was the year it took me three months to tear down the playhouse in the backyard.

This was the year a 30-pack of beer would not last two nights in our home.

This was the year the sweet gum tree died due to the drought. It was neither a young tree nor an old tree. It never looked like it was dying.

A lot of guys went door to door offering to remove dead trees. I hired Jim the Tree Guy to cut down the dead sweet gum. Jim was lean and tall, like a tree. He underbid the competition and I was persuaded by his confident moniker. And he made a flyer, which he kept folded in his back pocket. His jeans sagged like mine. Least I still had my teeth. I don't remember if I was drunk when I hired him.

This was the year I found a message on my wife's phone

that, in response to a question asking what are you doing, said undressing you with my mind.

This was the year I discovered the playhouse in the backyard was built better than our home. The previous owners, a couple from Minnesota, constructed the thing. Fuckers. They wanted a refuge in case of a blizzard, I guess. Or a nuclear war. We live in Oklahoma.

They believed screwing the half-inch plywood walls to the two-by-four studs was not sufficient. They added nails for security so that destruction of the walls required a meteor or a tornado. Or the combination of me, a sledge hammer, a crowbar, a bunch of beer, and a brand new ax.

It was educational. I learned that swinging a sixteen-pound sledge hammer is good exercise. It can also, when used during July and while drinking and after your wife changes lunch plans last minute and then cannot be reached by phone for the remainder of the afternoon, bring a person to a peak condition known as a heart attack. Or, fortunately in my case, an effective approximation of one.

This was the year I stood naked in front of a full-length mirror, squeezed my fading buttocks, and asked them why.

This was the year my wife turned on the passcode lock on her phone.

This was the year I discovered Jim the Tree Guy's assistant was his wife, who was far-sighted and did not like to be called Jane the Tree Girl. Jim didn't speak much when she was around. She wondered about the drought and the trees and God's plan. She told me it says plain as day in the Bible if you cannot see signs and wonders you will not believe.

I became aware of the sweat on my body. I wasn't wearing a shirt. I hadn't been wearing one all summer. I used to laugh at men my age who did yard work with no shirt.

I told her to make sure she didn't pull down the stop sign in my yard. Just the tree. Get it? I said fortunately the stop sign tells you to stop. It has the word right on it. I told her I wished other signs did that.

She said science was to blame. Science and insincerity. She

smirked. This must have been her favorite phrase. It was why she home-schooled her twelve-year-old daughter, who stayed in the truck until it was time to "tim-ber" the tree.

Jim didn't attend to the limbs or the branches. He said it was the tree I wanted down. Not the limbs and the branches.

He hacked a V-shape cut in the trunk with his chainsaw. He said this was easy. He wished we had more droughts.

Jim the Tree Guy couldn't remember how many trees he had cut down. He tied a rope around the trunk of the dead sweet gum then around the truck's trailer hitch. His wife got behind the wheel. The rope stretched but the tree didn't fall. Jim told her to stop but she didn't hear him.

The rope broke.

This was the year I discovered I couldn't predict the four-digit number of my wife's passcode lock. But I could bring her beers, wait for her to get a call, and then glance over her shoulder.

This was the year I hired a kid to help me tear down the playhouse and fired him within the first hour because he asked for too many breaks.

Later that day the father of the kid who had been hired to help me tear down the playhouse but not lasted an hour came into my back yard to complain about my language. I told him if he didn't like my way with words maybe we should have a different kind of conversation. I wasn't wearing a shirt and was standing beside a pile of beer cans. It was ten o'clock in the morning.

He didn't want to have any kind of different conversation with a man whose language he didn't appreciate in the first place. As I approached, I thought he was backpedaling so he could see me as he clarified his observation but after he had a hard time with the gate latch and then jogged, wordlessly, to his Nissan I understood that the starter pistol for his flight was the ax in my hand. I held the tool, which can be also be considered a weapon, over my head then flung it end over end at the sweet gum. The blade sunk into the heart of the trunk.

I held my arms aloft, sweat streaming down my ribs. I might have roared.

I wished my wife had seen. But, of course, she wasn't around and if I sent her a photo she would think the thing was staged.

I tore down a lot of playhouse that day.

This was the year my wife said she and Brad were just friends. It didn't matter that they worked together. She said they flirted on the phone because they were both struggling in their marriages. And no longer felt attractive because their partners neglected them. If not for the children, she said.

I told her we only had the one child. Didn't we?

This was the year my wife told me she was not going to allow me access to her phone or her email. No matter how many coffee cups I broke. Or beer bottles.

This was the year the rope around the sweet gum broke and the tree rocked back and forth. If it fell it was going to crash through our bedroom. I didn't whimper as I watched the tree rock back and forth because I thought it would be wonderfully ironic if a dead sweet gum crashed through our bedroom.

As it turned out, Jim the Tree Guy really was a tree guy. He hugged the sweet gum and it stopped rocking.

His daughter was still in the truck, shooting the scene so she could post it to YouTube. She was disappointed when the tree came to rest. Jane the Tree Girl wondered what was taking so long.

This was the year I began to conduct surveillance and discovered I was pretty good at it. I wondered if I should make a career change. I knew Brad's daily habits better than his wife, who didn't search her husband's phone.

I carried new binoculars under the seat of my car. In addition to the crowbar. And the ax.

My best friend told me that I could go to jail if I really hurt Brad.

This was the year Jim the Tree Guy said his prayers had been answered when the sweet gum didn't crush him to death or crash through our bedroom. He stretched his jaw and felt for blood on the side of his face that looked scalped from pressing against the bark. When I told him I never met a real tree hugger, he sucked one of his remaining teeth. I didn't mean to insult him.

He told me, as he was fashioning the rope higher on the tree, that prayer had worked once already so he was planning on using it again. Handing me the ax, he asked if I had a better idea. He was still hurt by my insult.

This was the year my wife told me that I had been angry or depressed for a long time. She showed me bank records with red circles around liquor store purchases. They went back and back. To the days when I still had an ass. But the circles grew like a contagious rash as she turned the pages forward.

This was the year I told Jim the Tree Guy a plan in addition to praying would be the best way to "tim-ber" the tree. I tossed the ax in the air and caught it. I did it again. Another trick I was proud of.

Jane the Tree Girl blared the horn when I asked for her opinion. Then I said some things to her I regret saying in front of her daughter, who was still shooting the scene with her phone.

This was the year I wanted to hatchet every phone.

This was the year Jim the Tree Guy began to unfashion the rope around the dead sweet gum, telling me he didn't want to work for atheists. I pushed the trunk of the sweet gum, intending to topple it on the space left by Jim's departing truck, hoping his daughter was still filming.

But the sweet gum listed toward the street and then began to rock back toward our house. When I saw the brake lights on Jim the Tree Guy's pickup I hoped he had changed his mind about atheists.

I dug my feet into the dry ground, braced myself against the falling tree, and prepared to die. I whimpered. I saw the lonely ax lying on the ground where it had been dropped by irony.

This was the year I discovered that my abundant desperation and my newly-acquired strength were enough to nudge the sweet gum past the house and onto the rubble of the torn-down playhouse. I was unconcerned with irony because it would have come at the price of me but I did note that the falling tree could have done to the playhouse in an instant what it took me three months to do.

This was the year I learned that a dead tree was not enough to teach me a lesson.

I drove to my wife's place of employment. But it was not her I was waiting for.

Her car was there but she didn't come out at five. Brad did.

I planned to cross the road to confront him but realized he could get in his car and lock the doors before I reached him.

I raced my car across two streets and skidded to a stop in the space beside him. He stopped as quickly on the sidewalk. My heart was swinging a sledge hammer in my head.

I wondered if the awful squeal of my braked tires had damaged my hearing but then I heard a girl crying. Brad's wife was in the car but she wasn't looking at me now or making a sound. His daughter was.

I moved closer to the window so I could see better, as if a different vantage point would change the view. Of me. Of this scene. It did.

My reflection appeared in the glass. The ax and crowbar in my hands, which I told myself I had brought for show, were positioned such that they flagged beside my head like ears. Donkey ears.

This was the year I lost my ass. Because I had become one.

This was the year, as I lay on the floor alone in my new apartment, I thought I could hear the wind sifting through the leaves of the sweet gum or the sound of children having fun in a playhouse. Or a wife talking to me at home.

This was the year when, though I lost my ass, it seemed for a while that with my new ears I could hear everything.

The Following is a Reenactment

Standing in the wings of *The Bill Sutton Show*, Melinda Simmons thought she heard a phone ring.

She knew there was no phone. No ringing. She turned to look anyway. She saw a dark wall. She saw the young, ponytailed assistant who was dressed in black, wearing a headset and holding an illuminated clipboard. State Senator Lori O'Bryant was reciting her lines, lint-rolling her purple sleeves.

The ringing was in her left ear. It wasn't a ringing. It was the vibration a ringing sound made. She told people when she made a call, held the phone to her right ear, she could hear the ringing in her left. Maybe feel the vibration of the ringing in her left was a better way to put it. No one believed her but they said they did. Either way, it was true.

Sweat broke on Melinda's forehead. She needed a towel. She shouldn't smear her make-up. She lowered her head to listen once more for the sound but didn't hear a phone. She heard her name.

She shouldn't do this. The assistant touched her wrist. The girl's fingers were cold. Melinda wanted to cry. The girl tugged her sleeve. Melinda walked as she had been instructed.

The stage lights did not allow for shadows. The polished wood of the padded chairs made her mindful of church pews. The blue screens on the wall were fluid yet stable, water in the baptismal.

She didn't dare glance at the audience, where sat her son, Colton, her mother and father, the dozen friends who had come for support. They were all eager to come. Times like these.

Worried she was not walking a straight line, she looked at Bill Sutton. She nearly extended a hand, to ask for help. He wore a navy blue suit and sky blue shirt. His tie was wine red with slanted stripes.

He had a mustache, like her father. Like Quentin. She and Courtney had made fun of mustaches. Quentin always got mad, but her father laughed, every time. Melinda smiled at the thought. Then, seeing Bill's solemn expression, she remembered her place. She was wrong to smile. She was here for Courtney. But she couldn't bear to think of Courtney. Or not think of her.

She continued her trip, head down, believing that with the next step she would collapse in a pool of tears. When she reached Bill, he touched her arm, to show compassion and to lift her face.

The cameras were pointed, like guns.

She waited while Bill talked to the audience. The stage lights were bright as a camera flash. She had been warned not to look at them, to look at Bill, pretend the audience wasn't there. But they were. They were the reason she had agreed to be on the show, to tell them her story, to let Senator O'Bryant offer her plea for change.

Melinda looked at the lights.

She couldn't see. She turned to Bill. She wanted to reach for him but knew she couldn't. She was supposed to stand and wait until he asked the question they had rehearsed. She was to explain why she had come on the show.

She squinted, trying to see through the white light. The blindness drained her balance and she fell. But more shocking than her descent to the floor was the return of the phone, ringing in her left ear.

***

When her senses returned, she was seated in one of the padded chairs. Bill was leaning over her, head turned. She saw his ear. Inside were tunnels, tiny hairs like winter grass on a ridgeline. A little world. Where no one knew.

Bill was waving someone toward them. All of Melinda's people were piled at the foot of the stage. Senator O'Bryant, who was kneeling on the other side of the chair, leaned closer, smiling. Melinda wanted to tell her she needed a new hairdo. Melinda could do that. She was a stylist. She didn't understand why women preferred such a cut. It was a female mullet. Courtney called it a permullet. There was a website.

Bill closed in, speaking. His teeth were stained. Melinda never noticed that on TV.

She straightened her posture, embarrassed. Everyone was looking at her.

She smiled at her concerned parents, mouthed the word, "Okay." She thought of asking Bill Sutton about the phone. He was a psychologist or something.

The pony-tailed girl was listening to a voice in her ear, relaying the concerns to Bill. There was talking and head shaking and talking and head nodding. Melinda heard them say they had the tapes. Could cut to them. But Bill maintained that someone had to be present, on-stage.

"The mother could fill in," the girl observed, touching her headset. "She's here."

"We need Melinda to get the law changed," Senator O'Bryant said. "This is her story."

They turned to Melinda, who said again she was okay, it was the lights. Could they turn them off? They laughed, relieved. And then there was silence as they waited for her to stand.

***

Melinda knew the events had occurred, but at times, could only remember them as they appeared on the tape Bill Sutton was planning to show. She decided her fear stemmed from the realization that she would have nothing to add. Or that people would think she just wanted on TV.

Senator O'Bryant had been at the funeral, called a week after that, was in her living room the next afternoon, hugging Melinda and her family, accepting coffee and pie from Melinda's mother, who was calling friends to tell them the state senator was there to show support and get the law changed. Friends brought over more food when they heard. There was so much Melinda's mother had set up TV trays in the living room.

Senator O'Bryant claimed something had to be done. The

story had to be told so that Quentin's actions wouldn't be the last word, so that another man couldn't do what he had done.

Melinda agreed, then she cried, wondering why Senator O'Bryant couldn't have arrived before it happened.

Three weeks later, a producer and camera crew were in Otto. Reenactment was the word. Everyone walked on it as if it were thin ice on a farm pond. But that didn't stop them.

The producer, a slender woman named Lena who wore as much makeup as a broadcaster, believed Melinda looked too good for the taping of the first abduction and insisted that she dress down and make her hair appear "winded."

Melinda began to muss her hair but was worried that she would look like a slob. Everyone would see.

Realizing that she was concerned with her hair when she should be thinking of Courtney, Melinda excused herself. She rushed down the hall, locking the bathroom door, where she prepared to vomit tears. But she didn't cry.

No one came to the door to inquire. Melinda looked in the mirror. She told her reflection that she was going to get through this. No one else could do it for her. She had to do this for Courtney. Senator O'Bryant was right. Melinda knew speaking aloud to herself might be a sign that she needed help but she was the only one who could understand.

When Melinda returned to the kitchen, Lena was complaining about a cricket in her hotel room, the lack of restaurants in town. Melinda's mother was sympathizing. She said friends kept bringing so much food. Lena doubted any of it was Lo-Cal. They stopped talking when they saw Melinda.

Lena was tall with a skinny neck and high cheekbones. Long hair would have been the first thought, yet she wore hers in an A-line bob. It made her features more severe but maybe she wanted them that way. The cut was perfect for work and outdoor settings, and she could tuck it back with a headband or even a pencil behind her ear.

Quentin would have been unable to take his eyes off Lena. She was the type who dominated his fantasies, the professional girl who couldn't control herself in his presence. When

Melinda's kids stayed with her parents, he had tried to get her to play dress-up, pin her layered cut back into a bun, wear a business suit. He had even bought a cheap black briefcase for the possibility, even though Melinda never consented.

If he had been at the taping, he would have driven to The Magic Bean and returned with a mochachino, which he would have handed to Lena and insisted she drink. He would have followed her, offering ideas. "I would think—"

His insistence would be too much for Lena to confront directly. Melinda wasn't the only one. Lena would resort to expressing her resistance through sarcastic remarks shared with the cameraman. Melinda's mother would have left the room. Quentin would glare at Lena, then ask if he could have a word, as if he were a colleague. He would whisper something to her no one else could hear. She wouldn't make another comment. She would apologize to him, explain her rude behavior as the result of stress. Quentin would crack a joke about her competence, loud enough for everyone to hear.

They would all be wary of him, thinking he had threatened the woman, wondering why she didn't have the courage to call him out. They would presume that they would have had the guts to counter the weird, inappropriate man if he challenged them. Silently, they would have thought these things while they watched him continue his strange blend of praise and harassment.

They wouldn't know that he hadn't threatened her at all. His tone would have been cold as a highway patrolman's, but he would have said something like, "I'd appreciate it if you didn't make fun of my speech impediment" or "I know, because I have Oppositional Defiant Disorder, that I don't always seem normal but it's made worse when an authority figure points it out in a crowd."

Quentin was a walking catalogue of disorders and diseases. Melinda thought his curiosity suitable, at first, because he was taking classes to become a nurse. He had done a lot of things in 37 years, knew about a lot more, the initial source of Melinda's attraction. His interest in history motivated her curiosity in the cultural development of a variety of hairstyles. But his fascination with the ill and disfigured didn't stop when it became clear he was making no progress on a degree.

She thought she had caught him with a bundle of bookmarked pages of porn on her laptop—the one he had appropriated for his studies—but instead of naked women she found photos of children with cleft palate.

The next week she made an appointment to speak with one of his instructors, an old school professor nicknamed "Bloody Mary" because of her ruthlessness as an evaluator. Melinda posed as Quentin's cousin. She didn't know why, realized as soon as she hung up the phone that something was very wrong with him or her or both.

She selected this professor because she had withdrawn Quentin from her course, but the administration reinstated him. According to Quentin, the Vice President knew what a bitch "Bloody Mary" was. It was time for her kind to retire.

But according to Dr. Mary Weir, Quentin was returned to her course because he was a paying customer. Schools were now run by businessmen, she said, who thought students were customers not adults who had to be mature enough to receive honest evaluations. Quentin Creed was, she told Melinda, manipulative, demeaning, and antisocial. "He needs help worse than most people who are receiving it," she said, peering at Melinda over her bifocals, which were held round her neck by a chain made of braided green and white yarn, school colors.

"But he seems so normal," Melinda said, as if she were attempting to retain her composure while a brown recluse spider scaled her leg.

"Does he? Really? Do you think intelligence is an excuse for meanness?"

"No," Melinda said, chuckling at Quentin's belief in his own brain power. He was so bright the professors didn't like the threat he posed to them in class, he said.

"He does. He doesn't say it in those words but he thinks he

knows better. Has he never told you how to behave?"

"Well, yeah, but I'm his, you know."

"He needled one student so persistently about facial hair she started shaving. I finally persuaded her to withdraw, make an appointment with a counselor. He only saw her three times a week, one class and a lab. Imagine if he were with her all day?"

Melinda burst into tears, an expression that now seemed to her as sudden and yet inevitable as a pregnant woman's water breaking.

Dr. Weir didn't offer Melinda a tissue or condolence. "Tell him to get help. Ostracize him if he refuses."

"What?"

"Shun him."

"Is that the best way?"

"With him, it'll be the only way."

She departed Dr. Weir's office before her tears were dry. She checked Courtney and Colton out of school, drove them to the Biscuit Hill restaurant, quiet at two o'clock in the afternoon, and made them start talking. Colton, quick to size things up, exaggerated Quentin's remarks to reward Melinda for taking him out of school early. But Courtney, who was quiet and intense, said things that made Melinda wonder why she had ever thought of herself as a good mother.

* * *

Bill Sutton was describing her story. His arm was around her shoulder. He had informed the audience before the cameras came back that her difficulty on-stage was a case of nerves. Simple stage fright, he said, building sympathy for her. He laughed and so did the audience.

He hugged her as he told the audience she was not to blame. He wanted to make that clear. She was the result of a fatal flaw in the law. They viewed the tape on the monitor.

Melinda watched herself park her Grand Am in the driveway, rushing home during her lunch break to set the DVR to record an episode of *One Life to Live*, a soap she and Courtney wanted to start watching again. For two years, they had given in to Quentin's constant ridicule of soap operas. He didn't like anything which wasn't "real," which he thought was staged and phony. The irony was that's exactly the way he wished life to be. But he wanted to be the one writing the script, starring in the show, directing the action.

It was hard to believe, seeing her house on TV. It didn't look like home. She looked phony walking to the door. She almost laughed, watching herself trying to walk casually and not look at the camera.

When Melinda entered the kitchen, the tape stopped. A photograph of Quentin she had taken appeared, a small square that grew larger. It was a close-up. He was smiling, but even when he was happy he looked harsh, and Melinda knew everyone would wonder why she had dated such a strange man. She remembered blaming the victim, when violence occurred, so she could be assured it wouldn't happen to her.

She had taken the photograph last Christmas but all the viewer could see was Quentin, no tree or presents. He had on his new brush-popper shirt, which he defended, claiming the classic look never went out of style. He had fashioned his mustache into the handlebar kind, which made him look spookier. He trimmed it with Melinda's best scissors every day.

While Bill Sutton's voice on the tape described Quentin Creed as a controlling individual who had dated Melinda Simmons off and on for two years, a montage of photographs, selected from Melinda's photo albums, faded in and out of the screen to illustrate the back story. Melinda was amazed how quickly the show had assembled these pieces into a story.

Things had gone well, at first, said Bill. Quentin had held a variety of jobs in his life but was clearly very intelligent. He'd never married. He flattered Melinda by telling her he'd never met a woman who enjoyed the lost art of conversation. Until her. He just needed direction, he said.

What Bill should have said, Melinda thought, was Quentin

had never met a woman who would let him do all the talking.

But the longer they dated, Bill continued, the more Quentin attempted to control the relationship. He even went so far as to prevent Melinda's children from seeing her parents. This wasn't completely true. Melinda wanted to speak but she couldn't interrupt the story.

Melinda had changed, Bill's voice said. She knew it was going to be hard to break a two-year habit. She took the kids to Oklahoma City for a weekend without telling Quentin, calling that night to say they were seeing old friends, claiming she told him. He just couldn't remember. He didn't believe her, accused her of cheating on him. When he began his explanation of how he had always known she was a whore, she hung up.

She didn't go to work on Monday, had her father change the locks. She called Quentin that afternoon to tell him she was breaking up. When it sank in, he cussed her, demanding an explanation. She turned her phone off.

Her parents spent the night with her, calling the police when Quentin wouldn't leave the driveway.

He frightened her but she refused to speak to him. She didn't want to identify reasons or describe his problems because his explanations would fatigue her to the point of acceptance. Refusing his calls, she realized how worn out and lazy and indifferent she had become. Working full-time and parenting active teenagers wore a person down so that, of an evening, she could put up with almost anyone sitting on the couch beside her at night, watching TV, so long as he didn't stink or run up the phone bill.

The audience heard this information from Melinda's taped voice, as photos continued to appear on-screen. She sounded relaxed. She had done the voice work after a long day of shooting. The audience was relieved to hear her make a joke. They laughed, for the last time during the show.

When Melinda filed a restraining order against him, Quentin didn't like it but he recognized a change had come, Bill said. He pretended to become part of the healing process, making an appointment with a biofeedback clinic for help with his moods. Melinda told him on the phone she was happy for him. She wished him well.

But he broke in, Bill said on-stage. The Christmas photo of Quentin returned to the screen. He waited, Bill continued, ambushing Melinda when she came home. He was better, he said. Melinda had loved him in the past. They were soul mates, and she knew it. She had asked him to change. He had changed, so now she had to take him back.

"But Melinda didn't see it this way," Bill said, sighing. The screen went black and the tape stopped. "She had moved on. Or so she thought." He hugged Melinda's shoulders. "Are you prepared...is this okay?"

Melinda didn't react. The stage went silent. She tried to take a step, do something to break the silence, but Bill held her on her spot.

"She knows it's hard but the right thing to do," Senator O'Bryant said, stepping toward them. She produced a tissue from her sleeve even though Melinda wasn't crying.

"Are you sure?" Bill asked Melinda. His breath smelled of pretzels and peppermint. Everyone waited.

Melinda nodded, twice.

Bill took a deep breath, looked at the floor, then turned to the audience. "At that point," Bill said. "Quentin Creed drew a gun."

Background music, odd and grating, blared as the images turned dark and grainy. Instead of normal action, the figures moved in slow motion, as if in a room with a strobe light.

"Melinda Simmons was about to be kidnapped," Bill's taped voice said when the music receded and a dark image of Melinda, a frightened look on her face, froze on-screen. The cameraman had captured that shot by startling her during a break. He apologized but she wondered if he did it on purpose. He knew his job. Of all the imagery she had seen on the tape, this one seemed the most genuine. "In her own home, a house she had purchased with savings she patiently tucked away working as a stylist at a beauty shop. This is a woman who had been through one divorce when her first husband cheated on her. But she had not felt sorry for herself. Receiving sporadic help from a deadbeat ex-husband, she worked long hours to provide a safe, comfortable life for her children. She had taken control of everything, except her personal life. And she was ready to do that. She didn't need a man to make her happy. But she deserved to find a mate who could be happy with her. Even her children, who were often caught up in their own busy lives, supported their mother in this change."

The music returned then ebbed quickly. "But when Melinda tried to leave, she was told that she wouldn't be going anywhere," Bill's voice continued. "Not until she changed her mind about breaking up with Quentin Creed."

Throughout the shooting of this part of the reenactment, Melinda kept thinking of ways she could have ripped the handgun from Quentin's grasp and shot him with it. She had trouble recalling details of the event, so Lena placed her in rooms and positions she assumed would have occurred. Melinda did remember that seeing Quentin with a gun didn't frighten her. As the cameraman gave her instructions, she couldn't understand why she hadn't just walked out the door, daring Quentin to pull the trigger. It seemed so possible for her, during the reenactment and now watching it, to change the outcome. She knew she did this every time she read about a violent story, telling herself and others what she would have done in the same situation so as to create a better result.

As she followed Lena's directions, she remembered a voice in her head had shouted at her to wake up. This man was crazy and threatening her with a gun. This was how people died, believing they couldn't be killed.

She did what Quentin said, wondering if she should act scared to make him feel powerful or less frightened so he wouldn't think he was in control. It was so much harder when you were involved because you didn't get to try it one way, see how it would turn out, then make changes. He didn't expect her home until five, which meant he planned to show Courtney and Colton his power. Melinda had caught him off-guard and he was struggling with his act. He would have planned everything out. He expected to have the afternoon to rehearse his approach, watching himself in the full-length mirror screwed to the closet door in her bedroom. The only time he ever hit her occurred when she accidentally surprised him at home, singing a Tim McGraw song as if he were in concert, looking into the mirror, his shirt off.

As Quentin lectured her, claiming the problem was she simply didn't understand him, he stole glances out the windows, peering nervously, too smart to be surprised by the police. But Melinda decided that what he was really doing was trying to hide his nervousness, buy time so he could think up his next line and his delivery. Whenever he gave her an instruction, he gestured casually with the gun as if he'd done this kind of thing all his life. It looked like a heavy weapon, a .357 with a wooden grip. Melinda wondered where he got it but didn't ask. Quentin was always coming up with things she didn't know about.

Her own Ladysmith .38 was in a tackle box under her bed.

Quentin knew she had a gun. When Melinda went to the bathroom, she walked down the hall to the one connected to her bedroom. He followed but didn't warn her. Melinda decided that he wouldn't have forgotten her gun and probably had taken it out of the box, hoping she would make a move for it so he could calmly laugh at her, demonstrating his foresight, like a smart villain in a movie.

"You looking for this?" he would ask, dangling her gun from an index finger.

Quentin was content to stay in the house all afternoon. He gave Melinda instructions on how she was to act once the kids got home. If she deviated from the script, he would produce the gun and bring them into it. She would come to her senses, eventually, about the importance of their relationship. But it would take a long time to regain his trust. He would have to remain in her home, day and night, armed, until she proved her faithfulness. If she brought someone home—her father or the police—he would go peacefully. But then he would return, and they would start back at square one.

Melinda didn't listen to this explanation because it was provided for the audience in her taped voice. She couldn't believe her accent. No one outside of her family would be able to sympathize with such a dumb hick.

The music and the jumpy images returned as Bill's voice explained that Quentin, frustrated, became violent, threatening to punish Melinda. He did say those things but they didn't lead to a "breaking point" as the story made it seem. They did this to make the phone call that saved her more dramatic.

Ginger Eberle, from the salon, called to find out why Melinda wasn't back from lunch. Penny Ingram was waiting for her perm.

The audience heard the call conducted by Ginger and Melinda, reproduced and read from scripts. Ginger overplayed her reaction at every turn but Lena finally got her to "bring it down."

Melinda explained to Quentin why she had to take the call. He allowed her to answer, the barrel of the gun pointed at her head, occasionally touching her temple and neck. Melinda watched this scene, surprised. She had forgotten that she allowed Lena to hold her own gun—which Quentin had forgotten about, meaning she could have dropped an earring beside her bed and shot him—to her head as she pretended to speak into the phone. Lena even nuzzled her face with it, a move she must have picked up from the kind of movie Quentin liked.

The girls at work had once talked about establishing a code word for occasions such as this but never followed through. Melinda couldn't remember any of the phrases they considered. She spoke slowly, allowing long pauses between answers. When Ginger asked if everything was okay, Melinda said fine, drawing the word out.

"Okay," Ginger replied, confused by Melinda's reticence. Ginger got this reaction right on the first take. She remained somber, out of respect for Melinda, but pride resonated when

Lena described the response as perfect. Ginger asked to use the bathroom. It took her five minutes because she called her family to tell them.

During the phone conversation, Melinda slowly explained why she had run home at lunch, even though Ginger knew the reason. Melinda talked about the soap opera, making up plotlines and questions, so she could keep Ginger on the line. She fooled Quentin with her feigned excitement; he couldn't contain his disapproval, groaning as he whispered at her to get off the damn phone. He lost sight of himself from his desire to explain to Melinda, which he did soon as she clicked off, how he might have some trouble with his moods but fantasies of the rich and famous on TV did far more social damage. It was a documented fact.

While he conveyed his insights, Ginger, sensing something was wrong with Melinda, phoned the police, offering a description of her car and directions to her home.

When two patrol cars arrived, Melinda felt her body sweat yet her mouth turned so dry she struggled to breathe. Agitated, Quentin paced the living room, stunned that his plan hadn't worked, trapped in his own disbelief. The rage in his face terrified Melinda but she didn't say a word or flinch, thinking the calm and the quiet would make it harder for him to pull the trigger.

Quentin bit his lips, thinking. Constantly calculating, he unloaded the gun, dropped the shells down a vent, and stashed the gun under the sofa. He opened the front door, acting surprised to see the officers, startled to see their guns drawn. He told them Melinda was inside. They had been debating their future. Relationship trouble. Normal problems. You know women.

Melinda was so relieved she fell into an officer's arms, asking him to take her away. The officer asked for her story. Addled, her account didn't make sense and Quentin laughed. See what I been dealing with, he said.

Finally, she was able to show them the gun and produce the word *kidnap*. They arrested Quentin. He accepted the handcuffs but his jaw was set so tightly he looked like he could chew through the metal.

"Her family and friends rallied around her," Bill's voice said as a scene played of Melinda in her living room, talking with her parents and co-workers. Melinda didn't want to cause any hurt feelings so she invited all of the stylists at the salon to be present in the room, even though only Ginger and Brandy Cartwright showed up after the actual kidnapping. As the scene played, no dialogue could be heard, which was a good thing. They looked so phony, pretending to describe their concerns and make plans. Melinda couldn't believe the show used it at all.

"But their relief was short-lived," Bill said. The tape stopped. The cameras were on him. "Sometimes, you're driving down the highway in your car and everything appears to be running fine. But suddenly it just dies. An undetected problem brings the whole thing to a stop. That's the sad truth for Melinda and Courtney Simmons. A fatal flaw in the law brought their lives to a sudden halt."

The tape resumed, showing Melinda frantically packing her car. Bill's voice explained that she had just received a call from the chief of police. He was alerting her to the imminent release of Quentin Creed on bond. Melinda was stunned.

"I couldn't understand how a man who had held me at gunpoint could be back on the streets within a matter of hours. I had done everything I could under the law. I had a protective order against him but that hadn't stopped him. And now the chief of police was calling and giving me his best advice, which was, 'Watch yourself. He's getting out.'"

Melinda didn't hear her voice offer this account. She was remembering the plans she'd made with Courtney before she left town, how calm and responsible and strong the girl was, how she told her mother everything was going to be all right. Courtney understood things Melinda could never grasp. She remembered watching the girl do her algebra homework, amazed. On summer nights, before Quentin entered their lives, Courtney would point out constellations and explain, once again, what a light year was, how space and time were intertwined.

Yet she remained pretty and popular, in spite of her brains. She was a cheerleader as well as captain of the debate and academic bowl teams. She received attention from boys, but she didn't seem to need them the way Melinda had. She was too smart for loneliness. She had won a scholarship to Oklahoma State. She would never get mixed up with a man like Quentin Creed.

Courtney reminded her mother that this wasn't her fault. She wasn't responsible for Quentin Creed's actions. Then she dared Melinda to ask Bill Sutton if he had his mustache dry-cleaned.

Somehow, Melinda knew that Bill had been explaining to the audience that no one believed she was safe as long as she remained in Otto. Quentin didn't know the identity of Melinda's friend in Oklahoma City. Her parents had agreed to look after the children.

But apparently Bill had asked her a question. Melinda wanted to tell him to wait a minute, she was talking to her daughter Courtney. The one this show was about?

No one said a word. Melinda hadn't heard the question and Bill refused to answer for her. "She thought if they were with her, they'd be in danger," Senator O'Bryant said, offering the answer she had helped Melinda rehearse. "She was the one in danger. She was the one he wanted to hurt. Everyone agreed."

Bill waited for the audience to quiet. Senator O'Bryant touched Melinda's shoulders. She wanted to shrug her off. "Is that right?" Bill asked.

Melinda looked at the cameras that were pointed at her.

"But Quentin Creed had other ideas. Including one," Bill said with an authority that suggested he wouldn't have been fooled, "that nobody suspected."

Melinda was startled by the sound of another ringing phone but this one played on the tape, which was showing, from a distance, a man rushing out of a pickup in the Otto High School parking lot, holding a gun. Melinda didn't watch the rest of the scene. She knew the man would force Courtney out of her car and into the pickup then speed off.

In Oklahoma City, Melinda had let every call go to voicemail unless she recognized the number. She changed all her ringtones to a downloaded old telephone ring. She turned the volume to the highest setting. Sleeping with the phone, she believed the loud ring would awaken her, in case her children or parents had to contact her in the middle of the night.

But this call was coming from Courtney's phone, at the time she normally got out of school. She wouldn't have cheerleading practice because there was a game that night. It was a home game, and Melinda planned to disguise herself and sneak into the stadium to watch the game and see her children.

Quentin was on the line.

Pastor Jesse Tolbert's voice, rough and loud, said, "This is Quentin. I've got your daughter." They altered it to make it sound even worse.

His voice continued but they lowered the volume because Pastor Tolbert wasn't very good. He sounded like someone reading lines. That wasn't how Quentin sounded. He told Melinda a lot of things as he drove out of town. She couldn't remember any of it, except his tone. He wasn't doing an awful thing. This was necessary. He sounded as if he was trying to control his emotions after learning he'd won the lottery, which the state was trying to take away because of a technicality.

Bill Sutton's voice explained what Quentin said to Melinda over the phone, lines written by Lena. He told Melinda this was her fault. But he was in control now.

Bill's voice described how Quentin followed a series of connecting section roads into the woods, how Melinda, afraid to get off the line, wrote frantic notes to the ten-year-old son of her friend who had just come home from school, how the boy called the Otto police, relaying Melinda's frightened message. But how none of them knew where Quentin and Courtney were located or where they were going.

The show slowed to the pace of a dying heartbeat. Melinda couldn't see anything but darkness beyond the bright stage lights. Bill's voice conveyed Quentin's trip down an old hunting road, following the turns of Salt Creek. He stopped the truck in the shade of black oak and witch hazel. He forced the girl out of the cab, walked her to the creek's edge, handing her the phone.

And then Courtney spoke. Melinda heard the fear and anguish in her daughter's voice but she assured her that there was nothing to worry about. She was there. It was all going to be over in a few more minutes. She didn't need to be afraid.

"I love you, Mama."

Melinda would have said, "I love you, too," but it was Shelby, Courtney's best friend, speaking. Why was Shelby talking? She hadn't made the trip.

And then no one was speaking. Bill was looking at her, lips pursed, a mournful expression on his face. Senator O'Bryant was crying.

Melinda turned to the audience but she still couldn't see anything. She couldn't see Courtney.

She continued to look for her as Bill quietly described how Quentin turned the gun on Courtney then himself. How he kept the phone line open so Melinda could hear the shots, how, afterward, she could only hear the sound of the running creek, the leaves in the wind.

Melinda didn't stop him because she knew he had to do this. He had to finish the story.

Melinda, squinting, looked into the audience. She found her son, her mother, her father. Her friends. Senator O'Bryant held the tissue to her face, shaking her head. Bill Sutton was looking at Melinda, the same concerned expression. Everyone in the audience was sniffling and staring at her.

The stage was silent. Melinda waited.

But Courtney wasn't coming on-stage.

Bill asked Melinda what she thought should be done. What could they do to address this fatal flaw?

Melinda held herself, tears filling her eyes. Her hands began to shake. Her chin trembled. She wanted to speak but she had nothing to say. She listened but she no longer heard

the ringing. All she could hear was the silence at the other end
of the line.

Bois d'Arc

There were two of them, standing thirty feet apart on the line, fixing fence. The sun was behind them, suspended a breath above the horizon, casting their shadows across the bar ditch, the dirt road, onto the waning pasture in forms that were stretched and unfamiliar.

Holding one end of the severed wire, Elbert Qualls leaned against a thick bois d'arc post while his grandson Billy attempted to join the splice. The boy was not a good worker, and he had been especially peevish today. He had thrown tools, kicked posts, asked for water every five minutes. He refused to wear a hat on his long hair or a shirt under his ragged overalls, so the heat and his sweat occupied him more than the work. He was now insisting on using the claw hammer and the fencing pliers to loop and bind the wire when one of the tools and some elbow grease would do.

The new strand sprang from his grasp before he could gain a kink in the union. Billy dropped the hammer, then the pliers. It had not rained in a month. A grasshopper's launch could kick up a scruff of dust. Billy stared at the tools, which had landed beside the come-along in the dirt at his feet, as if he looked hard enough they might undo their descent, float back to his hands.

Elbert took a step, then stopped. Even though Billy was 16 and most of his troubles were of his own making, Elbert wanted to help him out. He wasn't sure of the way. The kid's struggle had been made heavier two weeks ago by the death of his grandmother, Mary Katherine, Elbert's wife of 52 years. She had been the boy's mother since he was three.

Elbert's response to grief was to work longer days. That's why he had intentionally damaged his own fence, snapping the top wire in two places with cutters before dawn. There was no hay to cut or bale. The cattle were easy to call and count. Find the shade and you'd find them. Fence repair had greater urgency than tractor maintenance or tool arrangement, and stood a better chance of occupying Billy's time.

Elbert hadn't planned for the job to take all day. He'd expected to be done by early afternoon, then they could get out of the heat, attend to some things in the shady work barn with the big fan going. Maybe talk. But as they set about to repair the wire, they discovered a rotting post when Billy kicked it after snagging his leg on a barb. The section of fence wobbled so that Elbert could see there were other posts in the same predicament. These weaker posts were cedar. They were intermixed along the fence line with bois d'arc posts, jagged, mean legs that didn't rot, black as a mule's eye, hard as petrified wood. He knew he should replace the failing posts, but new cedar stands wouldn't look right among the gnarled bois d'arc. This fence line had been his for half a century, and the bois d'arc posts, which were older than his bones, would last another 50 years or more.

Instead of setting new posts, Elbert drove to town, mute Billy in the seat beside him, and bought a yard of gravel from the Dolese Brothers. He and Billy uprooted the posts, dug holes three times the needed size—working the post hole digger in time with Billy's bitching—and poured a mote of rock around the old posts to secure them. It worked, though even Billy had enough sense to question the legitimacy of this repair. From the road, the stoned posts looked like makeshift highway markers commemorating the dead.

Shoveling rock, Elbert's back seized up on him. He had to make Billy finish the job. There was a catch in his lower vertebrae that would not release, and every time he stepped, a raw iron of hot pain became his leg bone from the hip down. He gritted his teeth on the plug tobacco in his jaw to mask the anguish. The juice sluiced off his rough tongue, swimming among his gums.

The pain had not ebbed when Billy, still staring at the tools at his feet, observed he'd had enough for one day. Elbert said they were going to see the fence repair through, even if they had to work by way of flashlight. *Good luck with that*, was Billy's reply.

A black Chevy short-bed topped the hill, driving too fast,

glass packs clapping Billy from his self-absorbed stupor. Elbert recognized the truck and its driver. Damon Wisdom was son of the family that owned the adjacent farm. Impressed by their take the previous year, they had put up a fancy gate at their place, fashioned with the name of their ranch and their brand. They had replaced their fence lines with new aluminum wire and tamped metal posts that had been set too shallow in the sand and were headed for an early sag. They had doubled the size of their herd, though they didn't have the pasture to support it. They were only five years in and did not put back nor foresee the land's ability to take away more than it had given.

Damon was not made to work. He played baseball. In two years' time he and his father would be forced to employ the cleverness they now used in promoting his talent toward explaining his failure. At the moment, he was a hot shot and as proof he had pretty little Michelle Lowe beside him.

She had dated Billy several months ago. Now, wearing a polka dot bikini top, she flowered her fingers out the top of the window and waved as if she were letting go of cellophane. The funnel of dust in the truck's wake spread from the road, moping over the workers and their broken fence. Billy picked up a stone at his feet and made as if to throw it.

But he was acting, again. His life was a role he could neither accept nor make real. He saw Elbert glaring at him and then he got mad and threw the rock at the Wisdom pasture where it landed like a dull reflection and disappeared.

By this point Elbert was angrier than Billy. He had removed his gloves to wipe his face with a handkerchief and had not yet reseated them on his withered fingers. He wasn't sure why but when the pickup thundered past, he grabbed the wire for support and didn't let go even though his palm wrapped a barb. Watching the dust rush onto him, spread by a Wisdom across his wide field, his fence line, his livestock, he squeezed the barb, then placed his other hand on the wire cutters in his back pocket, eyeing the Wisdom fence.

Instead, he walked toward Billy who was staring at the

distant truck as if he'd missed his ride. Approaching, Elbert bit back the pain so that russet spittle slithered out the corner of his mouth and down his chin. When he spoke, he was startled by the volume of his own voice. He was barking at the boy. His leather boots slipped on a brittle patch of brown buffalo grass and he reached out to grab the wire. Tobacco juice had dribbled onto his checkered shirt and the blood from his hand had slid down his arm, falling onto the cuffs of his jeans which were stuffed into his boots. He looked as if he were preparing to lash Billy with the wire.

Startled, the boy leapt from the fence line. He cleared the ditch but landed awkwardly and went sprawling. He scrambled up, boots slick-spinning on the dirt road. When he saw Elbert wasn't coming, he stopped, rubbing the dust from his face as if it were the residue of everything he'd heard and seen the past five minutes. Then he turned and headed up the hill.

"All right. Now get on back. That won't do you any good. You gotta keep—" Elbert started to roll a sleeve but it had already been turned back twice. He wanted to give chase but it was futile. He wanted to ask Billy for help getting home but knew the boy would think he was faking. He picked up the hammer and the pliers and the come-along, groaning so loudly a steer forty yards away gave him the eye.

Elbert stared after his grandson. When Billy kept the same pace over the hill, Elbert turned back to the fence, shaking the tools free of dirt, shaking them still, as if they were acting crazy.

***

By the time Elbert got home, it was past dark. Billy wasn't in the house. At noon, Elbert had set out a pound of hamburger meat, wrapped in white butcher paper. The meat was soft, gray in places, but it didn't stink. The watery blood that filled the plate, dripping over the edge onto the green and gold Formica counter, had attracted a pair of flies.

There were no hamburger buns in the bread box. An empty package was on the counter beside a twist tie and a circuit of crumbs. Billy must have stuffed two of them with lunch meat on his way out, thrown the other two to the birds for spite. Elbert walked to the garage, but there were no buns in the freezer. Rummaging through the meat, his broad belt buckle pressing against the edge of the appliance so his belly wouldn't have to absorb the pressure, he located a package of frozen french fries. Mary Katherine must have bought it. The expiration date said the contents would no longer be at their best.

In the kitchen Elbert scooped the meat, unpeeled the wrapper, and dropped the lump into the cast iron skillet on the stovetop. He ripped the fry package open with his teeth, dumped a chunk of the crinkle cut potatoes, garnished with ice crystals, on top of the meat. He spun the lazy Susan until he located a can of pork and beans. He found pickles, mustard, and ketchup in the icebox. They went into the pan, along with the beans and two slices of American cheese. Elbert didn't know why he was doing this, but he turned the heat up on the burner. He opened the refrigerator once more. There wasn't much on the shelves, which were coated with ringed deposits and cold crumbs.

On the bottom stood twelve half-quart Mason jars of fruit preserves.

Elbert stared at them. Eleven of them didn't have to be in the refrigerator. The one that had been opened still contained nearly all of the preserves. Elbert reached for it, grunting to a cry as he bent low. The pain that had dulled from its persistence during the long walk home now announced its claim on Elbert once more. New sweat broke on his brow beneath the stand of his gray crew cut, free as a child's tearful torrent. Elbert pawed the moisture away, the back of his hand letting him know he might actually be crying. On most days, the man could still hoist and heave an alfalfa bale with one arm, and after he wrenched the lid from the jar and pried the sealer with his callused fingertips, he hurled them against the sunflower backsplash. He grabbed an unwashed spoon from the sink and turned the jar up, intending to dump the contents into the frying pan. But when he saw the slide begin, the first refined peach blob splattering in the greasy uncooked mess, he righted the jar and quickly spooned the fallen preserves back into the container, picking out the detritus from the jar with his fingers, piece by piece.

He touched the cool glass. He held the jar with one hand, then the other. He pressed the glass against his cheek, his dust-grimed neck. He looked again at the others on the bottom shelf of the icebox and then he unsnapped his shirt, placed the jar against his chest, pushing stuck sand grains aside. He could feel his heartbeat through the glass.

He took it with him to the table, where it sat beside him.

***

His dinner was terrible. The items never blended, even though they cooked in the same pan. Elbert gave most of it to the dog.

He was afraid to shower so he bathed himself with a wet washcloth. To swab his back he tossed a bath towel into the sink, mashing it down as the water from the faucet rose. He wrung the fabric, then tried to wipe his back with a side-to-side drying motion. But when he raised his hands clutching the ends of the towel over his head, as in victory, his back screamed and he dropped the towel, stumbling onto the counter. He gnawed an end of the towel, swallowing the water, then threw it against the hallway wall so it would stick and rubbed himself along its length, a dog straining to scratch an itch. He shouted as he did so. He cursed, twice.

He wanted to go look for Billy. The boy had come in the night before in a rush. He refused Elbert's questions, pinning his attention to the wall as he walked to the bathroom. He went straight to bed, an oddity unto itself, smelling as if he'd swallowed a tube of toothpaste. Elbert snuck into his room at four-thirty to confirm his suspicions. Billy's breath smelled of propane and peppermint. Another reason Elbert had roused him early to repair the fence.

But Elbert wasn't going anywhere tonight. He hoped to sit in front of the television, read from his Bible. Instead, he found the carpeted floor. Prone, his bones ceased their complaint but the muscles in his lower back throbbed, a fleshy puddle of heat and pulse.

Lying on the floor, Elbert tried to remember stories from the Old Testament to ease his pain. Battles, conquests. The lifeless sprawl of bodies on the mounds of sand.

***

Even though it was Friday night, Billy came home at half past ten. Elbert was asleep on the living room floor.

"Grandpa!" Billy cried. Dropping to his knees, he cross-hatched his hands, placing them on Elbert's chest.

"That's not where I'm distressed," Elbert said, slowly waking.

"Oh, God. I thought—"

"What're you doing home? What time is it?"

"Ten-thirty."

"Oh. I hoped it was morning."

"Go to bed. What are you doing out—"

"My back."

Elbert rose with a groan. Billy helped him to his feet, tried to lead him down the hall to his bedroom, but Elbert directed him toward the kitchen instead.

They went out the back door, looking like a hunched, three-legged beast, into an arc of yellow light afforded by the bell-shaped security lamp atop the pole that brought electrical and phone lines from the road to the house. Beside the pole stood the brick well house that Elbert had dug and framed in 1954.

The dog, Bandit, barked at them until Elbert spoke. Then it wagged its furry tail, watching. Billy led Elbert to the propane tank, a white capsule beside the well house. Elbert asked to be placed across it. The tank rang with a metallic echo when struck by Elbert's belt buckle. The old man removed the belt, then draped the long container like a lumpy rug. He asked Billy to climb aboard. Billy did so, sliding off the other side in his haste, asking if this is what he and Grandma did when they couldn't make the chiropractor's. Elbert grunted.

He liked the pressure on both sides of his spine, and when Billy found the right spot with his hands, Elbert let out a low moan. Billy worked harder than he had all day at the fence, and he didn't desist when Elbert's trousers began to slip from his hips.

Elbert told him to keep mashing. Billy did, pressing harder, even when Damon Wisdom's pickup appeared on the road and stopped, idling. The dark silhouette of the truck and a floating mesh of dust in the headlights was all that could be seen, but the volume of laughter suggested there were riders in the bed as well as the cab. A voice cried, "Faggots!" The laughter ignited.

"Up a notch," Elbert said to Billy. "Press."

On his knees atop the tank, Billy compressed Elbert's back with fingers and knuckles, working the flesh between the bones. The laughter swelled. Unheard jokes were voiced. Billy worked harder and Elbert's back popped. Elbert groaned and sighed. He slumped and went limp.

Billy hopped from the tank, trotting through the angular shadow of the well house to the gravel drive that circled through the property between the house and the barns. He picked up a stone. Elbert knew this time he would hurl it. With an audience, the Wisdom boy would have to respond.

He slid from the tank, feeling like a newborn calf, proud of its legs, wary of steps. "Son," he called. And when Billy looked, Elbert tugged his loose white underwear to his knees and bent over, showing the pickup of travelers the only moonshine he'd ever owned. It was Billy's turn to laugh, and he did so long after he had released the rock in his hand.

***

The next morning Elbert slept until five of eight. He hadn't slept that late since he'd contracted the flu in '87.

He walked carefully down the hall, stiff in the chamber of his remembered pain. He was going to let Billy sleep in. Maybe have the day off.

He wasn't hungry but he needed something on his stomach. He poured a glass of milk and made toast, setting the temperature too high. The slices came out charred on the crust and around the edges. Elbert didn't care.

He carried the Mason jar with him to the table and made himself open it and scoop a fat dollop of peach preserves with a spoon. Mary Katherine wouldn't want him admiring her work, as if in a museum. He ladled the fruit, which she had made from their well-tended orchard, onto the bread, piling it on. But before he brought the toast to his mouth, he spread the jam onto the slice with the back of the spoon. He layered it evenly toward the crust, thinning the fruit. He mashed the lumps, covering the toast with a smooth coat, pushing the excess back into the jar.

Then he ate the toast, bite by bite, letting the bread and jam dissolve in his mouth as much as be ground by his teeth. The blackened edge did not blend with the fruit as well as the browned grains of the center yet it tasted right. Ashy and sweet.

When he was done, he stared at the framed print of Jesus on the wall. He no longer wanted to ask why. He simply wanted to know what he was supposed to do.

***

When Elbert couldn't find the fence repair tools, he worked up a lather by the time he climbed into his flatbed truck and headed down the road toward the Wisdoms'. He was sure Damon and his cohorts had pilfered his tools, though that seemed overcompensation for the cost of a glimpse of an old man's ass. But such were the Wisdoms.

Elbert was even more surprised to discover that Damon had nothing to do with the disappearance of the tools. Billy had taken them and was at work, repairing the fence. A small water jug, the one with the leak, was at his feet. A red and white bandanna formed a headband and was already burgundy-spotted with sweat.

The line was straight and fine, but Elbert slid the truck to a stop and hustled out of the cab when he noticed that Billy had both hands on the come-along, straining to tighten the wire.

"Not a banjo you're stringing," Elbert said, chuckling to hide his concern. He pinched the wire. Tight as a new fan belt. The posts that formed the H brace at the corner were straining against the pressure. And then Elbert spied a bigger problem. Billy's ratchet job had jounced the weak cedar posts, springing them from the rock support.

He touched the boy's arm, not as a caution but as a stop sign, while he canvassed his brain for the right covey of words. He didn't want to trounce the boy's effort.

"You'd think I'd know better," Elbert said, retrieving the plug tobacco from his front pocket. He took his time liberating his pocket knife, which he kept so sharp it could slice a red hawk feather, separating the vane from the shaft, in a single pass. With the tip he pried off the plastic then cut the tight paper wrapper. He whittled a chew from the plug, all the while considering what he should know better.

"Rush a repair job and you'll do it twice. Happens every time," Elbert said, yoking up the sound of an old sage.

Billy followed his line of sight and spun around. "When did that happen?"

"Doesn't matter."

Billy removed the bandanna, wiped his eyes, squinted at the dangling posts. "Cattle can't get under that. Won't look right. I know, you don't like that but—"

"Could be all right. For a time. Maybe a long time. Cattle don't go looking for new holes." Elbert spat beside a horned toad in the ditch. "But if one leans against it." Elbert touched the tight wire. He couldn't help himself. He had to teach Billy as well as work with him.

"I thought it looked better this way," Billy said, bouncing his gloved fist on the top wire. "You mean, this is messed up? How I did it?"

"It's fine. Just don't have to be this tight to look good and do the job. Won't last as long as wire with a little play."

"Why don't I know that already?" Billy gazed at the cattle in the distance.

"Doesn't matter. What matters is what matters. Wanna go to town with me?"

"Why?"

"Get some new posts. That rock idea was a vagrant notion to begin with."

"You mean, we gotta redo it. I was almost done."

"You don't have to. Was planning to give you the day off anyway. Compensate for all your chiropractic work last night."

Billy smiled, wiped his face again. "How's your back?"

"Better."

"Happen a lot?"

"Some. More than it used to."

Elbert stepped down into the soft ditch, taking his time to mount the road. Billy walked down the fence line. He stopped at a bois d'arc post, tapping the top before punching it lightly.

"Leave the tools. Won't take me long," Elbert said.

"Why don't we replace those cedar with bois d'arc?"

"Don't have any bois d'arc on our land. Cedar around here not big enough."

"So you're gonna buy some?"

Elbert nodded and shrugged. "No choice. Come on if you're coming. It's already too hot."

"Someone's bound to have bois d'arc," Billy said, jumping onto the road, jogging toward Elbert. "Tree's gotta grow somewhere. New posts won't look good. Not on this line."

"I'm sure it does. You wanna take a week and conduct a survey?"

"I could."

"Lord."

"No one you know? We only need three posts. One good stout limb."

"Wisdom's got 'em. Down there on Salt Creek."

"There we go."

"Uh-huh. No, thank you. He tried to charge me when I asked to borrow a head chute last spring. For one afternoon."

"We could pay him for the whole tree. We'll need extra. There's gotta be other posts on that back forty in the same shape."

"Once he knows we want it, he'll call around and find the wood's valuable. By next Saturday he'll be running a public auction."

"So you don't think he knows."

"I know he doesn't. I cut myself a limb last year to make a walking stick."

"Why don't you use it?"

"Makes me feel old."

Billy climbed into the cab, but when Elbert tried to put the truck into gear, back up, and turn around, Billy grabbed his hand, told him to put it into first. The boy then pointed in the direction of Salt Creek.

***

The dirt road cut a path through the valley between acres of land that rose in abrupt cliffs and fell in jagged ravines, pastures that were too uneven for hay but fine for cattle. Elbert guided the flatbed toward the shaky bridge at the basin, where on both sides of the road tree lines marked the turns of the creek bed.

He parked thirty yards from the creek and walked the tools to a section of his fence that needed attention. He scattered the tools along the line, then snapped a crimper on the top wire for no reason. Billy watched in awe.

Elbert told him to be quiet and look. He glanced up and down the dirt road before pointing out the trio of bois d'arc trees on Wisdom's land. The trees' rise from the ground was a sport of hard bark and rough surge and arthritic branches, wielding a stubborn, contorted form, pinpointed by the map of their fallen fruit, a large, rough, rotund ball known as an Osage Orange or horse apple. The cattle would only sniff and nudge the stippled fruit. Even horses didn't like it.

He told Billy to find the third tree, focus on the thick dead limb and the long live one above it. The uneven display of branches and limbs from the trunk made the bois d'arc an easy climb. Billy was to get himself into position, then hoist the chainsaw up by rope. He would cut from the top of the limb down. Elbert insisted he move the blade side-to-side but stay on the top of the wood. He would be tempted to come up and under, but a missed thrust from that angle would send him off the back of the tree, clutching a cutting machine.

Elbert's voice grew in caution and distrust as he spoke, and he had himself talked out of this idea by the time he finished. But Billy, chainsaw in hand, rope dragging the ground, was already on his way.

The boy's abilities were engaged by the plan, and Elbert wondered why he hadn't seen such a tactic as a motivational tool years before. He let the boy reach the short, rusted bridge, then, leaving the wire crimper on, picked up the come-along and headed down the fence line in the same direction.

Elbert's breath quickened as he watched his grandson slip through the strands of Wisdom's barbed wire and tote the saw to the third bois d'arc tree. The plan was to let the boy attempt to scale the trunk on his own. If he couldn't, Elbert would slip over and help him up, then return to the imaginary work on his own line.

The boy took to the work as if he were fulfilling a long-forgotten dream. He and the saw were aboard the tree before Elbert could worry about his climb. Elbert quickened his pace to the creek, shrugging off his back's muted complaints about the faults it remembered from the previous day.

When he reached the shadows of the tree line, the plug tobacco suddenly dry in his jaw, he found that Billy was not only atop the tree but cutting, working the saw as if he knew from experience.

Elbert was pleased with himself and his planning. He gazed across the spread of his land, the source of his family's survival, and was tempted to give into the vanity of thinking about what it all might mean.

Then he saw Jack Wisdom's Dodge truck barreling down the road toward them.

Elbert took off his worn ball cap to form the preconceived signal but Billy wasn't looking. He didn't know whether to let Jack pass and hope he didn't notice or flag him down in the road as a distraction. Jack drove faster than his son, which was no surprise, but Elbert feared the sound of the saw would give them away, so he dropped to a knee and made as if he were struggling for breath in the ditch as the truck approached, hoping Billy would look his way before Jack got there.

The ploy worked. The sight of Elbert stooping caught Billy's attention and the gnawing hum of the chainsaw ceased. Jack stopped. He zipped the passenger side window down and called to Elbert. The man wore a cowboy hat as if he thought he were a big Texan. He had his radio going. The ram hood ornament on his oversized maroon truck gleamed in the sunlight.

"You all right, old timer?"

"Just had to catch my breath."

"Looks like you were doing more than that." Jack's voice was hard to hear above the whir of his air conditioning. He turned the radio down.

"Just about done. Thanks for stopping."

"Heard you were having some trouble keeping your pants up last night."

"My back," Elbert said, halting. "You could teach your boy some..." He ground the tobacco with his teeth, urging himself to let go the need of a righteous point and a drawn-out conversation.

"Lucky I don't call the sheriff. But I know you and him go back. Wouldn't do any good."

"Thanks, again."

"Sorry about your wife. That was unexpected. Wasn't it?"

"Your wife sent a card."

"Things are gonna get tough for you, Elbert. You want me and the boys to take over? Sure we could work something out."

"You must be worried about the lack of grass on your pasture."

"You never—" Jack paused. His tan, wizened face, stretched tight by too much sun and secret concern about his debt, cinched hard for a second. "We got plenty of hay," he said. He exhaled as if he'd been holding his breath.

Elbert could hear him put the truck into gear but he couldn't resist. "What are you gonna use this winter then?"

The transmission barked against its driver's impatience. "Like I said."

He bolted in a huff of dust, and before he reached the top of the hill, Billy gripped the handle and pulled the short cord of the starter until the saw throttled back to life.

It was Elbert's turn to watch in awe as Billy matriculated the tool through the radius of tough wood. The dead one bit back harder against the blade than the live one but neither proved to be an easy cut. Elbert wanted to be of more assistance, but he'd already provided the help he could give. Watching for intruders was his job. Standing under the tree would only distract Billy and narrow the perspective of Elbert's view if, in fact, the boy did fall.

It was the limb that dropped not Billy. The curled leaves cushioned the impact of its descent. The fruit, green as new hay, big as a softball, landed with a pocked thud on the ground. A pleasing sound, somehow. A comfort.

Billy removed the hand ax from the denim loop of his overalls and whacked up the cut end to make it look broken not sawed. Elbert didn't move until Billy had the long limb at the Wisdom fence. The boy shot glances down the road and called, "If you think I can javelin this thing over, you do need to see a doctor."

Elbert's grin could not unwind itself as he aided Billy's

effort. Once the limbs were on the metal flatbed, the tools were gathered, and they were both in the cab, they waited, as if they were players in a game they didn't want to end.

"That should give three posts, don't you think?" Billy asked, wiping his face with his bandanna. He chugged water from his jug, what was left of it.

"Mm-hmm. Use the dead one. Let the other cure."

"Wouldn't hurt to have more." Billy paused. "Would it?"

"Don't see how it could hurt, no."

So they took two more limbs, one from each tree. Instead of whining and tired, Billy bounced into the road when he was done, swishing broken branches in the dirt road as they dragged the last limb across, to cover their tracks, he joked. The stack of their load made them look like veteran tree trimmers. Elbert had to hook and chuck a strand of leather bungee cords over the branches and leaves for Billy to secure on the flatbed's other side. And then they drove home.

***

They spent the rest of the day trimming branches, measuring and cutting the limbs, then setting their new posts. Billy cut the wire so they could reset it and it whipped and flailed at them and they were lucky not to bleed. They laughed about it.

That night, Elbert drove them to town for dinner. Elbert ate sirloin and Billy ate chicken fry and they both ate mashed potatoes and Texas toast and salad and fried okra. Billy couldn't get enough, and when they were done, he reared back in his chair as if he had completed the warm-up and was ready for the real meal.

Smiling, Elbert said he thought he'd been dreaming when he saw that Billy had started to work on the fence that morning before he did. Billy lamented his tightening of the wire, but Elbert buffeted him, saying if he hadn't put in such initiative they would have never found themselves with new bois d'arc posts.

Then Billy's face turned. Elbert thought he'd embarrassed the boy and he started to speak but Billy leaned forward, putting his chair's four legs back on the diner's tile floor. "Grandpa, how did you know you wanted to be a farmer?"

Elbert looked at the boy, then shook his head, chuckling, his eyes dancing a strange jig in their weathered sockets. The variation of sunshine and rain, lightness and seriousness, in an adolescent's life was more mysterious than anything the weather had ever thrown at him. "I don't know. My father worked the oil field. I tried it but I didn't like the mess and the machinery. There was nothing alive in it, 'cept for the men, and I didn't like what the work did to them. My father was gone a lot. Made him hard and bitter. He drank. Maybe," he said, laughing, draining the dregs of his iced tea, "I picked farming because all you had to do to get to work was step out your back door."

"You're good at it."

"Well, now."

"You are. You see so far down the road when it comes to problems. Grandma told me no matter how bad things got or how low cattle prices fell, she never fretted because she knew you'd figure it out."

Elbert's lips pursed. He licked the top one, then he swallowed the saliva that was accumulating in his mouth. "I guess I knew that, but a man doesn't do anyone good thinking highly of himself." Elbert paused. He tapped free a thin ice cube from the bottom of the glass. "I'm glad you told me. I often wondered what you two were always talking about."

Billy took a deep breath, staring at the floor, as if he were a doctor sent to convey bad news. He said for the first time in his life he'd learned something he already knew.

"I don't want to farm," he said.

"Who's asking? Why would you..." Elbert said. Billy took another breath. "You did good work today."

"I know. I helped. I really did help. But that's all I can do. All I will ever—"

"You think too much, son."

"No, I don't," Billy said, looking up. "What I'm supposed to do. It's what you do."

"No one in this here café is holding a gun to your head, far as I can see. You've got all the time in the world to decide what—"

"I start my last year of high school Monday."

"Okay."

"But then that year will end. And I—"

"What?"

"Nothing." Billy imitated Elbert without realizing it, seeking the bottom of his tea glass.

"A man learns as he does," Elbert said. "There's no other way. No other teacher. You think you should know before you ever get started."

"I get that. You're right. I didn't but I do now. But that's not. As much time as I've. If I wanted to do this, I would already know so much more than I do. I can see things after you've pointed them out, but I don't see them until you do because I don't want to. Sometimes, you have to be able to see ahead and…"

Elbert was a breath from asking Billy what he really wanted to do but then it dawned on him. His concern wasn't just for his future. It was for his own.

The silence of the diner became a known thing between them. Sound of dishes in the back. An old couple asked a waitress if they could share a slice of pie.

"Want some dessert?" Elbert asked.

Billy shrugged, then shook his head. Elbert collected the check and paid it. He slid a toothpick into his mouth, offering Billy one, which he declined. The boy was sinking back into his silent self.

They passed the small public library as they neared the end of Main Street. Mrs. Greenstreet was locking up and Elbert whipped his flatbed into the parking lot so abruptly Billy's head knocked the window.

"I'm gonna get me a book on backs. One thing I don't

begin to understand and it's causing me more trouble than six miles of fence line."

He slid out of the cab without extending an invitation but Billy caught up with him before he'd entered the darkened foyer. Mrs. Greenstreet, yawning, was delighted by their interest, told them to take their time.

They checked two books, one for kids on the spinal column, Elbert joking that maybe it was one he could understand, and a thicker volume on human anatomy. When Elbert pulled into the roadside store for gas, Billy had both books in his lap, one propped open. After he filled his tank, Elbert purchased a half-gallon of vanilla ice cream and a bottle of chocolate syrup and before the dust in their driveway could settle, Billy was licking the sides of his bowl, which he had overfilled, and heading down the hall with ice cream and the books to his bedroom.

Elbert knew what he was to do. He plunged a spoon into the ice cream but he declined the syrup in favor of the Mason jar of peach preserves. Carting it and his bowl, he walked out the back door and eased himself down to the porch swing, where he and Mary Katherine liked to watch songbirds of the morning or a pretty sunset. He was going to work Billy like he had never been worked before. They were going to use Wisdom's wood and change out every cedar post for bois d'arc, restring the wire so that they would have a fence line that would last past 2050. They were going to buy more cattle, lease more land than they owned, bale more hay, and then before Wisdom went belly up and had to sell at auction, Elbert would place the house and the land on the market. This way he could let go of Billy and help him in more ways than by cosigning a loan. It was their place, his and Mary Katherine's, not his alone, and now she was gone, so he would buy a little house in town and play dominoes at the center. He'd save a limb or two of the bois d'arc for himself and make walking sticks he could showcase at the fair. And maybe some days he'd walk to the library and come home with a book on how barbed wire changed the wild west.

And when he got home, he'd open the icebox and take out a Mason jar of peach preserves, the lid crusty from age, and he'd smell the rich fruit and take the smallest of tastes, a sweet kiss, then close the jar and admire it before he clutched it to his chest.

Bear's Brother

Bear's brother turned off Highway 99 onto a long, bent finger of dirt road that wandered away from the marked asphalt and into the trees. He drove slowly, kicking up a commotion of gravel that pinged the oil pan and muffler, dust that lingered in the road before dispersing across the fence lines.

After twenty minutes of intersecting roads, Bear's brother stopped the car in a shallow draw beside a mulberry tree. There was no shade or shadow. The sky was gray. He no longer saw pastures or cattle or fence lines. Here, the land belonged to snarls of trees whose branches fought for room like antlers of bound deer.

Bear's brown trailer was a hundred yards away, wedged between two blackjacks and a box elder. A black satellite dish, wide as the trailer, stood in front. Bear's brother could see Lenora's red short-bed pickup. He could not see Bear's white one-ton.

The deputy's patrol car did not appear until twenty-five minutes later. The car drove past the tamped grassy entrance to the driveway. The deputy stopped the car, started to back up, then seeing a parked car in the road, pulled forward until he could look into the driver's window.

Bear's brother identified himself to Patty Grimes, who recognized him. He told them he was there to witness the effects of his actions.

"This isn't your doing," Patty said. "And it's not a final action. In fact—"

"It is a step that requires a holster and gun," Bear's brother said. He told the deputy Bear wasn't home so he probably wouldn't need the gun. He told him to take the safety off, though.

The deputy backed the car up the hill. He drove down the long driveway and stopped beside the pickup. Bear's brother followed, keeping his car in the road.

The deputy did not require the use of his handgun. He did require the assistance of Bear's brother.

Lenora shoved Patty Grimes off the trailer's rotting porch. Bear's brother saw Patty's thick, blonde hair rising as she fell. He also saw the deputy flailing in front of the patrol car as he tried to remove Lenora's fingers from his short-cropped hair.

Lenora did not let go until Bear's brother knocked the air out of her with a forearm to her back. While Lenora hacked for oxygen on her hands and knees, the deputy moved to draw his gun, then hesitated.

Picking up his hat, he yelled at Patty, directing her to get the children. She was still on the ground, leaning against the porch's bottom step, blood coming from her nose. Bear's brother rushed up the steps and into the fetid living room. He found the boys in their bedroom, the oldest, seven-year-old Randon, pumping his pellet gun.

Bear's brother told them he would take them to safety.

"Why's the sheriff?" Randon asked.

Bear's brother didn't answer. When he tightened his grip on Randon's arm, the boy tried to jerk away. Bear's brother ripped the gun from his nephew's hands and tossed it on the bed. Five-year-old C.J. held his arm up. Bear's brother took him by the hand, and led the boys down the steps.

Patty was dabbing blood with her fingers. The deputy was standing beside Lenora, gun pointed, holding his handcuffs. Seeing the children, he swung open the patrol car's rear door. Bear's brother ushered the boys to the car and did not respond when C.J. asked, "Uncle Tim?"

He closed the door behind them. The deputy looked as if he wanted to kick Lenora in the ribs. He dropped the handcuffs, picked them up, and said, "Let's go," to Patty Grimes.

After the car was gone, Bear's brother looked at Lenora, letting her know he made the call. She didn't give him a chance. She ran at him, screaming, one breast bouncing free from her half-buttoned blouse.

She punched him in the side of the head. He pushed her,

then made a fist. He didn't say a word as he walked toward his compact car, which he bought, reluctantly, for his 45-mile commute to the Hitachi factory in Norman. It looked puny and weak beside the truck. Lenora called after him, said he would wish for death once Bear found out.

***

Bear's brother waited for his encounter with Bear as if he knew the valves of his heart would close and commence an attack. He sat all evening in a sky-blue recliner with no burn holes in it, fingering a stack of plywood he and his wife had raided from a construction site to make the signs she sold at the local craft mall. Many of these signs hung on their trailer's paneled walls: *Tim & Bobbie's Nest, Watermelons 5¢, Free Hugs.* These signs shared the walls in equal numbers with the framed Home Furnishing decorations of birds and flowers Bobbie used to sell.

She never asked him to describe what happened. He didn't offer. She didn't ask him to help with dinner or cut a sign or paint one.

Bear's brother's leg twitched. Every two minutes, he took a deep breath.

"You don't need to stew," she said, above the sounds of the television and the frying cube steak. "This is for the best. He'll see that."

Bear's brother did not place a weapon beside his chair. Bear had hit him but never beat him, as he had their first stepfather when he slapped their mother, and David Wisdom for stealing five grams of crank on New Year's Eve, and Rocky Hughes for telling him he shouldn't be drinking beer at a little league game, and Leith Speers because he was from Vanoss and called Bear a pussy. When Bear got riled, he didn't stop until he expelled the worst of his anger, the other man unable to stand.

Bear's brother did not want to think about the pain, but he was not afraid to take a beating from Bear. He hoped Bear

-50-

would come by. He wanted to tell him what he had done and why he had done it.

When he heard a pickup door shut, he walked to the front door, opened it, and stepped out. The truck belonged to a neighbor. Bear's brother closed the trailer door, and sat on the porch until dinner was ready.

***

At 14, Bear's Brother went to work for Bear on a drilling rig. He bought his own car, a '68 Dodge Duster, paid for his own insurance, bought his own clothes and most of his food, so his mother could spend her paycheck on the younger kids. Later, he paid for three semesters of college, where he met Bobbie, made the down payment on her car and the trailer, which now sat on a landscaped lot in the Green Acres Trailer Park in Otto.

Bear chided his brother for going civilized. Still, they were family, and Bear always offered him a beer when he saw him, though it came with a joke.

With Bear for a brother, you could not be anything but Bear's brother. They had one sister between them, but no one called her Bear's sister, and two half-brothers and one half-sister beneath them, but Bear was more of an uncle to them. Bear could lift the front end of his pickup off the ground, snap a pair of pliers in two, shake a Volkswagen out of gear. Once, he lifted a fallen stand of drill pipe off a man's leg, which made him legend in the oil patch.

If asked, Bear would grant permission to a stranger to borrow money, eat his food, drink his beer, smoke his pot, crash at his house, or, as the jokes went but never near his presence, sleep with his wife. As long as Bear lived in Otto, his trailer was the center of the world for fifty people who all had homes. The cops knew what went on in Bear's trailer, but they never broached his yard. He talked with them when they cruised the trailer park. They liked Bear, joked with him, and knew, without being able to say it, that he created an order they could never provide.

That night in bed, Bear's brother lay on the mattress as if drunk. Any sudden motion, he sensed, would send him toppling over the edge. He listened to his wife's breathing, trying to find a rhythm in it he could adopt as his own.

He could feel the sheet on the hairs of his arms. His feet, constricted by the weight of the bedspread and the tightly-tucked sheet, strained and kicked until they felt relief. But, moments later, they felt, once again, confined.

***

Bear didn't call or come by the next day. Bear's brother picked up the phone, dialed the number, but no one answered. He called Patty Grimes. She told him the boys had been placed with a foster family, Mike and Tina Drucker, who had taken care of foster children for ten years. The word *placed* stuck in Bear's brother's mind. His nephews, who noodled catfish long as their legs, shot water moccasins and snapping turtles, climbed to the top of tall cottonwood where they spit streams of tobacco, were now files in a cabinet.

"They won't replace their parents," Patty consoled. "Mike and Tina will show support and faith in families, including your nephews and their parents. They won't promise they will be reunited, but they will show hope."

"Sounds like they've been well-trained."

"Parents need training."

"Like dogs, I guess."

"Tim," she said. "You called us."

***

After he caught Lenora with another man for the second time, Bear's brother sat in their trailer, looking.

He knew Bear was working twelve days on, two off, drilling for Thompson and Sons. Bear's brother wanted to take his nephews fishing. No one had answered the phone for two days. He was surprised to see the unknown black Jimmy parked beside Lenora's pickup. He was surprised by the lack of a response to his knocking. Then he was surprised by his surprise when, after he started calling the boys' names, Lenora let the trailer door swing open. She stared at him with a baffling expression on her face, a swarm of snarl, disgust, and crazy leer. She watched so much television and smoked so much pot there was no telling what vague scene might be playing in her mind, and what role she might be cast in.

A man appeared in the doorway. Tall, shirtless, he was fastening a big rodeo belt buckle strapped to a pair of stiff Wranglers. He had dark curly hair, long in the back, and a trim beard. "Who the fuck are you?" he asked.

Bear's brother looked toward the woods, searching for the boys he now hoped hadn't heard his calling, feeling his pulse tick. "You're trespassing."

"I'm the one inside, dickhead."

"You're the one gonna take a beating. And after I tell Bear…" His voice trailed off. This was Bear's wife the guy was screwing so it was natural to bring Bear into this. But he knew he was using Bear's name as a threat, something he had never done, because he wasn't sure he could take this man.

"What's he care?" the man asked.

"Let's wait around and ask him."

Lenora mumbled. The guy turned away from the door, then reappeared with a Zippo lighter, a pack of Marlboros, and a sandwich bag containing a small amount of marijuana in his hands. "She told me she was his sister," he said, bounding down the stairs. "I carry a .38 in my truck."

Bear's brother didn't think of the boys as he sat on Bear's denim divan with cushions sprayed with so many dark oval burns they looked like roly-polies on the underside of a wide rock. He didn't listen to Lenora's ranting excuses and accusations, but instead smelled the damp stench, thick as the sweat on Bear's palm, of diesel, oil, and pot smoke. The basin of an ash tray on the coffee table was overwhelmed with ash and butts, which spilled onto the lacquered table. Boots, caps, and torn copies of *People* magazine and *TV Guide* were strewn about the room. The brown and tan carpet, worn to the pad in front of the television, was sprayed with debris—pebbles, dirt clods, pot stems and seeds, crumbs from the crunchy breading on chicken fried steak and onion rings—and would have to be swept with a broom before the vacuum was turned on.

The wobbly kitchen table was stacked with dishes holding scabby pools of ketchup, french fries, chicken bones, and ribs that could be a week or two months old. Busch beer and Dr. Pepper cans teetered near the edge. Bear's brother knew there would be roaches and mouse droppings sprinkled on the table and the counter.

He heard the gurgling of bong water. Lenora was drawing a deep hit. He lit a cigarette. He didn't know how much time had passed since she quit talking.

Bear's brother thought of his nephews. They hadn't heard him call, were probably deep in the woods, wading through a creek or peering around a tree, drawing a bead on a grackle. He thought of them wrestling on the floor with Bear, rolling about like bird dog pups in a dusty pen.

He and Bear grew up in a home that was dirty compared with some of their friends, whose stainless, orderly rooms did not look lived in. Their mother, who managed a U-Tote-Em convenience store, left two husbands, and buried one, their father. She would not have approved of the condition of Bear's home, but she never entered it. She wouldn't have said anything if she had. It was Bear's.

Bear's brother preferred his mother's form of love to the constant suspicion and overprotection of other parents. But, sitting in Bear's trailer, he saw a blindness in his mother's acceptance, a blindness he had inherited when it came to looking at Bear. Now, every spot, stain, scrap, and ash spiraled back to the boys, who liked mud more than water, but were not dogs.

Lenora inhaled the scorched bud into the bong's filthy basin, releasing a funnel of smoke thick and long as her forearm. She walked toward Bear's brother, her lids lowered, mouth ajar, shoulder dipped. Stopping, she cocked her hip and fingered the plastic button of her thin, blue, floral blouse. Bear's brother could see the swell of her breasts and the lacy fringe of her bra. "Can I have a drag?" she asked.

"You want one?"

"I want yours."

He wanted to see how stupid she would get. Taking the cigarette from him, she didn't stroke his hand as he thought, but instead licked the filter before she put it in her mouth and made the fire glow with her inhale. He wanted to work his hands into her hair and pull, punish her by making her do the very thing that pissed him off. He took a short breath, and resisted an urge to kick the coffee table over. He and Bobbie made love the way frightened parents did. He thought it was warm and loving once upon a time. Now it was predictable and infrequent.

"Bear won't believe you," Lenora said, sitting, firing another cigarette. "And I got ways of persuading him."

Bear's brother turned and left without a word, hoping the silence would have some effect.

***

Patty Grimes told Bear's brother on the phone that her on-site visit to Bear's house—she called him Keith—had gone very well. The trailer had been thoroughly cleaned. The living room and kitchen appeared neat and safe, livable. Both parents, she said, seemed to understand that this was not a life choice but a health issue. The boys could not be returned to an environment that would put their well-being in jeopardy.

"What did Bear say?"

"He didn't speak. Lenora did all the talking. I think this has been good for her. For them both. She appeared understanding."

"Good," he said.

"Keith has cut his hair and shaved his beard. He has also

scheduled an appointment with the dentist to repair his teeth."

"You made him do that?"

"Of course not. But they're good signs."

"What happens now?"

"I'll make another visit in two weeks. Inspect the place again. If things go well, and I don't see why they won't, and Keith and Lenora attend the required parenting skills classes, then the children will be returned to their custody."

"And what if they don't go to the classes?"

"The boys will remain with the Druckers."

"How long?"

"There's no way to say. Until the parents demonstrate they will provide adequate care or until we decide they are unfit. But don't be alarmed. We aren't here to break up families."

"I know."

"If you could do anything, try to make sure they attend those classes. You might scoff at them, but they help, even when people are made to go."

"How are the boys?"

"Quite a handful, aren't they? They're fine."

"Why don't you let them come stay with me?"

"That's not a good idea."

That night, Bobbie, who hadn't spoken of the matter since the boys were taken, reassured Bear's brother. In bed, she came on to him for the first time in a year. Bear's brother put his body through the motions, but he felt like the fluff on a cottonwood, waiting to be taken by the wind.

***

After he interrupted Lenora with the wavy-haired man, Bear's Brother drove to the trailer every evening, kept his car parked in the road and watched. Bear was working the daylight shift, 6:30 to 2:30, driving 90 miles one way, but having to stay and work doubles, covering for the evening crew, until the tool pusher could find a replacement.

On the second night, Lenora climbed into her pickup and braked beside his parked car.

"Going to the store. Want something?" she asked. Her hair was done, and she was wearing a new black leather jacket. "Sweet of you to watch the boys for me?"

"Where are they?" he asked as she drove off. He hadn't seen them since he arrived.

He drove to the trailer, waiting inside. The boys came in at nine, three hours after dark, despite his continuous calling. Lenora didn't show until after midnight.

When Bear got off doubles, Bear's brother met him at the trailer one evening, asked if he wanted to go drink a beer. Bear and the boys were examining two arrowheads C.J. found in the woods.

"I wish I was Indian," C.J. said, drawing a bead with an imaginary bow and arrow.

"He couldn't kill a possum," Randon said.

"Could too!"

"You'd both damn sure haul ass if you saw a buffalo. Big as a bull," Bear said, standing. "Wide as this damn trailer. You get one arrow in, it wouldn't twitch. You'd have to chase it down, put five more in just to get it to blink. Watch it turn and charge your ass." He took a heavy step toward Randon, laughed when he fell backward.

"I'd pull out my knife," C.J. said, reaching down to an imaginary blade strapped to his leg. "And slit its throat."

Bear burst into laughter. "You'd piss your moccasins." He rustled the kid's hair, then put him into a headlock and rubbed his scalp with his knuckles until the boy complained. "That buffalo'd grind you into owl shit!"

Lenora, her eyes heavy and bloodshot as she stared at *Lifestyles of the Rich and Famous*, gave Bear a wet kiss on his way out the door, asked him to take the boys with him and pick up some cigarettes.

The boys scrambled into the back of Bear's truck, and after Bear's brother bought a six-pack at Jersey Lily's, they meandered deeper into the woods, under the branches of oak and hackberry. Bear told him he could have gotten twelve Busch for the same price, then talked about the new mud man's passion for handguns as he peered into the dense brush and thin trunks of saplings and dogwood, looking for turkeys. Bear was going to get one this year.

Bear's brother didn't speak. Bear didn't notice his reticence for some time, then finally said, "Bobbie must have warped your head with all that home decoration. You're treating that beer like it's your first piece of pussy."

"Fuck off," Bear's brother replied, taking a long drink. "Least she'll wash a dish."

Bear chuckled. "She take over your job?"

Bear's brother didn't want to proceed. "Somebody needs to make it their job."

Bear tapped the brake but kept going. "We get back, I'll put some rubber gloves on you."

"I came by the other night. She didn't roll in 'til midnight."

"She said you watched the boys. Shame Bobbie's too high and mighty to come out."

"Bear, I think she's—"

"What?"

"The place is a goddamn mess. Enough rat turds in the kitchen to fill a cereal bowl."

Bear eased on the brakes. "What?" He put the transmission in park. "Wha'd you say?" At every thought, Bear's brother heard Bear's reply before he could say it. The engine idled. He saw Bear's hand go hard on the seat, but when he raised it, he jerked the gear shift into drive and sped off, boys falling to the bed of the pickup. Bear didn't say a word, took the beer into the trailer with him, slamming the door.

***

Mike and Tina Drucker lived in a two-story frame house on a spacious but rough acreage, two miles off the highway. Mike was the principal at Briar, a K-8 school fifteen miles east. Tina taught English at Levi. They had a daughter, still at home, a senior, who was helping them with the Lehman boys.

Happy to see his Uncle Tim, C.J. ran back upstairs to retrieve the clay volcano he and Tina had made, which poured out real lava.

Randon stared at his uncle.

Mike was at school. Tina brought Bear's brother a glass of iced tea. He declined a piece of fudge. She was trying to get sick of the stuff, she said, before the holidays arrived so she wouldn't eat so much. She was a bright, dauntless woman, youthful in spite of the thirty pounds she didn't need.

"They've been so good, I'm gonna hate to see them go."

"Yeah."

"Things just get mixed up sometimes. Your car breaks down, and you need a new alternator or thermostat, and then you get one, and off you go. I told Keith and Lenora that."

"How did Bear act?"

"He wouldn't come in, which was fine. He didn't want to get out of the pickup, but Mike told him we were honest folk who reported everything to Patty, and did he want to make the mistake of putting the boys in the pickup cab with him? When he was this close to getting them?" She broke off, and looked at Randon. "You want something, sweetie?" He didn't reply. "Anyhow," she continued, "Bear talked with them from the cab, then got out for a minute. Boy, he's big."

"That's why they call him Bear," C.J. said, struggling with the weight of the volcano he slid onto the newspaper-covered coffee table.

"Shut up 'fore I make you eat that volcano," Randon snapped.

"Now, Randon, honey."

"Whyontcha come out tomorrow when my dad's here."

"Maybe I will," Bear's brother said.

C.J. poured the colored baking soda and vinegar into the dingy purple mouth of the volcano, and in a few minutes the eruption began. "Isn't that cool, Uncle Tim?"

"Yeah. Sure is." He looked toward Randon, who was no longer in the room. They heard the back door open and shut.

"Let's go outside," Tina said.

Bear's brother patted C.J. on the head.

Outside, he quickened his pace to catch up with Tina, turning the back corner of the house. A wishing well, made more than likely by some high school kids in shop class, and a long swing hanging from wooden supports flanked one another underneath a mimosa tree, the sloping pasture in the background.

Randon was throwing rocks at the silver propane tank, the ping echoing in the metal cylinder. "Randon!" Bear's brother yelled.

Tina, standing beside the well, held up her hand. Bear's brother watched his nephew, then glanced into the well. Bobbie would have one of these in a back yard of their own someday. It was new, the wood unweathered, and empty.

"It's all right," Tina said. "I only came out here cause he ran off Thursday night, after his folks were here. Thank goodness Mike's in shape. That little booger can scamper through some woods. Ain't afraid of nothing."

Another ping clamored, making a high piercing sound within the dull cavern, a shot fired in a tunnel.

"Shouldn't you take him somewhere?"

"Could. I probably shouldn't have told you. I told him he could call his parents, but Mike wouldn't let him. He didn't want to reward him for running off. Mike's the thinker. He knows all that cognitive psychology. He told Randon we could take him to the juvenile center. Other kids would be there, but we would insist Randon could not join them for anything. He'd stay in a room by himself all day. The food, Mike said, would be worse than he ever had at school. Then Mike asked him if this would make his father mad enough to do something. If he did, both Randon and C.J. would end up back in the juvenile center, maybe for six months or longer. Did he want his brother to have to go through that?"

Bear's brother watched the boy fire another rock at the tank. "He'll stay," he said. "That's what Bear would do."

***

In a dim twilight, Bear's brother drove down the dirt road to Bear's house. He allowed the small car to coast as he approached the base of the small hill marked by the mulberry tree. He nearly stopped beside it, but knew if he did, he would turn around. Shifting the car into first, he drove at an even pace to Bear's driveway, and turned down it, so low to the ground he felt as if he was mowing grass.

He stopped before he was halfway to the trailer, pulled the car into the rougher ground off the path, and parked beside a cedar and dogwood sapling. He was not here to make a get-away, but he could not draw closer to Bear's pickup.

He felt fear at the thought of Bear, but he knew he had done the right thing, even though it was family and though it was hard to put the word *right* beside his actions. The initial child welfare visits hadn't done any good, and Bear refused to recognize their authority until they finally removed the boys. Slapping the car door shut, Bear's brother strode toward the trailer, rounding Lenora's pickup when the trailer door flew open.

Lenora appeared, laughing. "Well, come on, dumb ass," she said, without looking back. "Don't forget your pen and paper." She took a long drag off the cigarette, watched the white smoke assert itself, for a moment, against the darkness.

Bear stumbled out. The porch groaned but didn't rock under his weight. "Got my goddamn dunce cap."

Lenora sensed a presence, and turned suddenly at the top step. "Well, son-of-a-bitch."

She skipped down the blunt steps, and charged in a rapid walk, flipping her cigarette against the trailer. It connected with a thump, launching a small shower of orange sparks.

Bear's brother stopped in front of Bear's pickup. Eyes on Lenora, he heard the jingling of Bear's overall clasps, and saw Bear's hand snare the shoulder of Lenora's flannel jacket. "Let me have him first!" she shouted.

Bear threw her against the pickup. "Get in!" She didn't. He

opened the door, grabbed her by the neck, and shoved her into the cab.

The door ajar, Lenora righted herself on the seat. "Tear him a new one. Make that pussy—"

"Shut up!"

Bear's brother relaxed. He was going to fight back, but his body held no fury.

Bear stared at him. Then he got into the cab and shut the door. Lenora asked what the fuck was wrong with him. Bear didn't reply. She continued to rant. He started the engine, and slid the truck into gear.

Bear's brother went stiff, arms tensed. Bear let the truck roll forward until the bumper hit his brother's knees. A foot on the brake, he slid the transmission into park and waited, revving the engine with a slow but loud progression.

Tim waited for Bear to emerge. Instead, he saw a man named Keith staring past him at the road as he held his screaming wife by the arm. Tim stepped aside, so the man, who would not look at him, could drive to class, continue the lesson that might allow the return of his children. Tim watched him go, then walked to his car without looking back.

Hook Echo

Caleb and Lyndsie Fisher were used to responding to problems, even those they couldn't solve. He was Operations Pastor and she was Experience Team Song Director for the Life Church in Daggs, Oklahoma. They made daily decisions that affected the lives of their congregation's 400 members, choices that determined the who, what, when and where of physical and spiritual union, more than the how or the why. Yet the familiarity of this involvement opened the door to questions from their brothers and sisters in Christ they couldn't answer so much as certify as sincere, legitimate, and godly.

Their authority on uncertain matters was elevated by their success. They weren't rich or career-driven, but they were attractive, trendy, and photogenic. They posted selfies that looked natural and cool because they had given everything to God, including self-doubt. Their style seemed to be a new revelation of their professional calling, where contact with a higher power allowed them to upscale distressed jeans, beard stubble, messy hair, hoodies, and leggings into a tony sanctuary that brought the high and the low together.

They often drew doubletakes as if they might be celebrities. There were so many now it was hard to be sure. No one mistook them for Hollywood or Nashville but they might be regional travel influencers or TikTok DIY home renovation trendsetters who favored decorative hangings and sashay fabrics that could be found at the intersection of HOA and Farmhouse Chic. He was buff with a cocked head and an impish half-grin (the other half had been straightened by God). She was form-fitting bounty and organic spritz and loose curls with a V-shaped arm on her hip and a smile white as a limelight hydrangea.

So when the Fishers walked into Will Rogers World Airport, passing a bronze statue of the man who was famous for many things, including death in a plane crash, then crossing through the shadow of *Prayer*, a sculpture of an anonymous Indian man in robe and headdress with arms extended and head lifted, they were noticed, and this attention grew as they sat at Gate 7 with a host of other passengers, waiting to board an airplane that was worm-holed to the jetway yet 90 minutes late in departure. For an unspecified reason.

Anxiety born of the delay was amplified by an event from the previous day, when the lead singer of a celebrated band, whose members still lived in OKC, put the entire place on lockdown after TSA spied a hand grenade in his carry-on. It was art, though few would have guessed without the designation, in spite of the yellow paint, and the guy turned it into an elaborate and comical production, similar in many ways to the band's stage shows. It couldn't explode, he sort-of sang, but if it did it would shower everyone with glitter! Every flight was delayed, coming in and going out, for six hours. Some passengers soared anyway through social media attention but most were not pleased and their frustrations seemed to join the concerns of those seated at Gate 7 with the Fishers, the way a cap of warm air will hold rising storms in the atmosphere until it can no longer withstand the compounding pressures.

There was stirring and mumbling. Sighing, moaning, and questions to the gate attendants and other passengers and the unresponsive air. Some of these queries hoped to be directed to various uniformed employees who walked to and from the jetway, shaking heads down to show it wasn't their problem to solve yet their striding pace revealed they heard the unvoiced complaints and were walking through the terminal as fast as they could to find someone who might know what to do.

When a portly woman with a neck as bulbous as a toad's struggled to breath, her eyes bugging as if the jetway was a vacuum hose sucking the terminal's oxygen, the Fishers decided to act. While others launched a search for a paper sack or a person trained in CPR, they prayed.

Caleb took Lyndsie's hand and delivered his salutation to God, but then she surprised him and the others seated at Gate 7. Raising one arm at a time, fingers extended the way she lifted them on stage at church, as if she were not only reaching for God but with Him holding the sky, she led Caleb into a surrender pose formation that looked more like the gesture of an antenna transmitter than a resigned human soul.

"God is good," she said.

He smiled. "All the time."

"All the time," she said louder.

"God is good."

As they repeated the mantra, a few others joined them. On the third round, half of the passengers at Gate 7 were speaking with a single tongue. The other half were smirking. One muttered, "He would hear you better if we were 30,000 feet off the ground."

The only unity, it seemed, could be located in the use of phones to record and share the experience. This activity occupied them all for a half hour, slowing the rate of complaints for the next. When a gate attendant announced that they could now begin boarding, amidst the cheering and congratulating, the woman who had been on the verge of hyperventilation put down her paper sack and walked.

She was one of many who thanked the Fishers as they moved toward the plane like congregants heeding the invitation song. The line of passengers was single file and the entrance to the bridge didn't look wide enough for two people. But the Fishers entered together, their phones still pinging with notifications, walking side by side through the blind chute to the cabin of the plane, as if they were following a path that had been privately revealed for them.

After they exchanged amens with an attendant who wore a flashing *He Is Risen* button on her lapel, they went down the narrow aisle, trying not to bump their carry-ons against seated passengers. The airline didn't assign seats. There was a row of three on each side of the aisle. It was a full flight so they couldn't expect a row to themselves.

Lyndsie led the way. She planned to walk to the back in order to find the best seats but then she heard her name. To one side was a full row of passengers who were on their phones, plugged into headsets. The other row contained a man at the window. He appeared to be asleep, the only person who wasn't buzzed with excitement. He had too much hair combed back, poorly held by his gel. His tie had been removed and stuffed into his coat pocket so that it looked like a dying corsage. He had on running shoes and a duffel bag in his lap that looked too big for its contents. Like him, it looked saggy and poorly assembled.

But he wore a nice pinstripe suit and a shirt the color of an Easter lily, mostly white but stained yellow under the collar. Lyndsie pretended to lose her balance and fall into the row. She caught herself on an armrest and paused so she could detect his odor before she made a choice. He smelled of starch and a memory of bleach. And he was leaning against the wall, which would give her more room. She raised her carry-on and popped it into the overhead bin, a move she completed with knee skills from her years as a cheerleader who served on the base of the pyramid. As she slipped into the middle seat, she forgot about hearing her name.

"This where you want to sit?" Caleb asked. He looked up and down the aisle, so he could join her consent. He took his seat and snapped a selfie of them. Many members of their congregation didn't travel much, some had never been on a plane, and would worry if the Fishers didn't provide regular updates. But the story of the Lord's rescue from the lengthy delay delivered by way of the Fishers was already spreading (one member who had seen the video likened Caleb to Moses leading them out of bondage; he couldn't identify the role Lyndsie had played) and the notoriety pushed for acknowledgment from the celebrated couple as if they were spiritual first responders in a world of secular emergencies.

The stranger at the window seat began to make abbreviated sounds as if he were dreaming. But his arm on the rest was too tense for sleep and twitched as if someone were stabbing at him with a knife that was nicking his flesh. Perspiration pustuled his face. He wiped it with his sleeve. He had to be nervous about flying. Lyndsie wanted to change seats but it was too late.

She had tissue in her purse but it would take the whole pack to wipe his forehead. She dug through the loose contents searching for a napkin she knew she didn't have. When he made the sound of a small dog moaning in its sleep, his discomfort wafted from the fabric of his seat into hers like a swarm of dust motes rising with the charged air before a thunderstorm.

His bag looked empty yet he secured his grip on it while she placed her purse on the floor. She couldn't help look and was startled when his eyes opened.

They made eye contact, which added to their difficulty. His face was half-shaven. The right side was razor burned but the cheek near the window sported three days' growth. He offered a nervous laugh, but even his chuckle was labored. "Guess I must be scared."

"First time?"

"No."

She felt a fear that reminded her of a child who has been left alone in Walmart. In response, she didn't turn to the surrender pose. She kept her eyes open and focused her mind on an emergency call to God: she wished to open a streaming line of prayer for the strange man, one that might induce a heavenly sedative.

"I have but I'm a little nervous, too," she said. "Always feels like the first time." She laughed, too loudly. Smiling, Caleb looked to see if he was missing something. He knew how to make things run smoothly. He patted her arm in relief. But before he could speak his phone bleeped and he returned his attention to his thumbs and the device.

The man was staring out the window even though the shade was only half-drawn. "Glad I didn't let them handle my things."

"I know. I saw them when I was waiting to get on the plane." She asked immediate forgiveness for her white lie. But she believed God would have done the same to calm this man.

"I'm not sure it would be any different if they were women.

Did you see that flight attendant when you came on? She should change her name to Phony."

He laughed and she felt as if she might become small enough to disappear behind her purse. A large drop of sweat slid down her ribcage, raising goosebumps in its wake.

He groaned, peering over the other passengers for a glimpse of the attendant. "Always something to hide."

As she took a deep breath, she wondered if she should tell Caleb or the attendant or just get off the plane. But the stranger was suffering. Running from trouble was not what they did. It's not what He would do.

"You could close the window shade," she said. "That might help." He turned and stared at the window. "I think it's that plastic pull down thing. You push down on that tab."

She placed her purse on the floor and reached for the window. But from the angle of her approach, it appeared as if her hand was aimed at his duffel bag.

"No!" he shouted, grabbing her wrist with a pressure that caused her to cry out. She had to tug her hand twice before he let go.

"Hey, now!" Caleb said.

A person in the row in front of them turned to look.

"I'm sorry. I'm very sorry," the stranger said, lifting the bag carefully by the handles as if he was not only checking the contents but their weight. "I thought—"

"I shouldn't presume," she said. "I wondered if the window might—"

"I need to look out."

"But the blind."

He turned once more to the halfway window without explanation.

"You know," Caleb said, unbuckling his seat belt so he could lean in. "It's much safer to fly than drive. I know a lot of people who have died in car wrecks but none in planes. Even tornadoes, like the one we just had, are more—"

"How many people do you know who own a plane?" the man snapped. In response to his own question, his eyebrows and mouth formed a smirk, as if positioned by wires, and his lips released a shot of air.

She thought she heard him apologize as he tried to turn from them. But the limits of his seat restrained his resistance against the confinement of the row. When he propped himself against the back of his seat, as if he hoped to push it to a complete recline by force, his face rose to the color of pink sandstone. The perspiration returned. He struggled to swallow and then appeared to be panting before he was able to catch a breath and hold it.

Caleb looked down the aisle for a flight attendant, then waited for Lyndsie to turn to him so he could say more with his face than the troubled man had with his. As if the unity that joined believer and non-believer was not their common humanity but their understanding that the key to the game of life was winning it.

But Lyndsie didn't turn to him. She continued to look at the man, the half-blinded window and the bag in his lap his arms were protecting like security guards.

When he spoke, he lowered his voice: "Know what you're trying to do. Don't waste your breath. I'm not worth it."

He wiped his face with his bunched tie.

Caleb held her hand then remembered her wrist. He examined it and asked if she was okay. She nodded. He asked if she wanted to move. She shook her head.

"Guess we're being tested for wanting a second honeymoon," he said. "You think Pastor Dennis had anything to do with this? Wait two hours to get on the plane and now we gotta go through this before we even leave the gate."

"We should pray for him," she whispered. "Something's gone wrong."

"Or something's been wrong."

"Do you really think sound can't travel the length of two seats?" the stranger said, calmly. His eyes were closed and he pressed his skull against the headrest.

Caleb nudged her arm twice to show her the message he had typed on his phone. *What's in his bag?*

She shrugged as his hands became the wings of a plane that descended below the bend of his knees and then exploded into a widening O that separated, drifted, cooled, and died. She rolled her eyes unconvincingly, reflexively reaching for the phone inside her purse. For comfort, for distraction, for videos of herself and her band performing at church. But then she thought she heard her name again and lowered the reflecting screen in her hands.

The strange man's eyes were closed but his lids twitched as if his head held tiny people who were trying to escape. He breathed with a regular rhythm that included a deep, sudden uptake of air every third inhale.

The slumped top of the duffel suggested there might only be one thing in the bag, something that could tumble to either end from a simple lifting. He wouldn't bring a bomb onto a plane and not try to disguise it. He couldn't bring a bomb onto a plane and not get caught. And the duffel was unzipped, the flaps forced out. So the contents could always be in sight?

She stretched in several directions as she tried to gain a glimpse inside the bag. When that failed, she became concerned with the buckle on an ankle strap of her block-heeled sandals, while she listened for the sound of a ticking timer.

She recognized the ridiculousness of her actions at the same moment that Caleb leaned over to gain a glimpse. The back of her head cracked his chin, tipping her hat back like a lid. His anguished groan was leavened with a laugh from the stranger. He blinked, as if he wasn't certain if he'd been amused by something inside his head or outside it.

The expression on Lyndsie's face mannered him. "I'm sorry." His eyes didn't want to be open or closed. "My wife..."

"She couldn't come?" she asked. Caleb pulled back, holding his chin, but was more wounded by her interest in the troubled man, as if his pain should always rate higher than the habits of a wacko, even if he was a lost sinner who might be reclaimed without too much effort.

The stranger was amused, then as quickly, appeared sick.

"She passed." The words fumbled out like a baby's spit-up. "Not long." He sighed then swallowed with great difficulty. "Can't tell if I'm rising or falling."

She gave Caleb an *I told you so* look as the plane lurched, as if a parking brake had been stuck, then backed away from the airport. The captain apologized but hoped a good tailwind would help them make up a little time. The stranger's chuckle at the comment became a full-blown laugh which became a coughing fit.

She handed him her pack of tissue while attendants demonstrated emergency procedures. The woman with the flashing *He Is Risen* button was closest to their aisle but the stranger didn't pay her any attention. He stared at the seat in front of him, though his eyes were fixed as if they no longer worked.

After the attendants concluded their demonstration of the tools required in case of a loss of cabin pressure, Caleb reversed the stranger's upstaging antics by praying. He lifted his voice so it could be heard but kept it gentle so as not to demand. It didn't rise or drop in response to the snickers from the row in front of them. Several passengers became aware of the prayer, if not from the words from the cadence. Caleb was well-practiced and well-versed. Though some people were still talking, the plane felt much quieter when he was done. Two people said, "Amen." Another muttered, "We heard you the first time."

She reached out and placed a hand on the stranger's arm. It jerked from the touch, as if the wiring was faulty. The muscles tightened and didn't let go their hold. But he let her hand remain.

As they approached liftoff, the breathy rush of sound made by the wind and the engines filled the cabin like a heavenly chorus that could be heard but never understood. It wasn't until they joined the clouds that the stranger thanked them for their prayers, even though he didn't need them. He wasn't lonely. "My wife is always with me. When we reach our cruising altitude, and I know we're safe, I'll let you meet her."

She pulled back and Caleb mashed his lips. Then he started a count he couldn't keep. "Hey, pal," he said, the cheer in his expression packed and stowed. "I'm gonna need to ask you a favor."

"All any of us will ever be remembered as."

"Even if you're somehow joking about this, it's not funny. Life is a serious business."

"Joking? You think I'm joking?" He opened the duffel bag with an economy of movement that was so rehearsed it had become natural. His efficiency prevented any panic. The sagging nylon sides collapsed as he let it slide to the floor while he removed a small bag that he placed on his knee as if it were a toddler. "Like you to meet my wife."

"Okay, now."

"I'm not kidding," he said, staring Caleb into silence. "Life is serious business. It's really her." He held a black velvet bag with a golden drawstring. Size of a five-pound bag of flour, it was cinched around a gray plastic sack that was secured with a stout twist tie long as a handlebar mustache. The corners of the sack formed a jagged crown and the crinkling that accompanied its movement made it seem alive.

"Gotta watch it," the man said, patting one side. "She can be a little flighty."

Caleb laughed in exasperation, and then, so everyone who heard his prayer thanking God for the precious gift of life would know, turned the sound into a scoff. "Look. We can sympathize but—"

She gave him a look that rivaled the stranger's glare. Turning, she said, patting the man's arm. "We are so sorry for your loss.'"

"Lyndsie," Caleb said. "Don't. I'm getting someone."

"You're kidding. That's your name?" the stranger asked, nudging her elbow so that it fell from the armrest, the left side of her body collapsing for a second like the duffel bag. He hoisted then plopped the velvet bag onto her lap. It felt like a sack of sugar that had bits of hard candy on the bottom. "Meet your namesake. Lyndsie? Meet Lindsey."

She held it with both hands, but once she knew its name she brought her knees together so the thing couldn't slip between her thighs.

"Feels alive, doesn't it? Like a doll. The longer you're with it. You know?"

She sensed that it wanted to be bounced, and when she saw she was about to comply, her fair face turned to stone.

"She's got a heft you don't expect. But her BMI is fine. She goes four pounds, three ounces. Hasn't varied. She's very consistent. Course, I don't know if altitude has any effect on her weight. I'm sure it does. Einstein showed us that space and time are one and the same. Which becomes a giant monkey wrench for any description of an afterlife where only one is present."

Caleb was gesturing to the attendant but she was taking drink orders several aisles away and motioned as if she would get to him soon. Lyndsie stared at the bag, as if fears deeper than a terrorized plane had surfaced.

"No longer has to worry about fitting into her clothes. Starting another diet. Stay awake wondering about one of her students who hasn't been at school in a week. We always had plans for trips in the summer but then she'd get committed to camps and tutoring and private lessons to keep kids from falling behind. So," he said, sighing as if he weren't relieving stress but hoping to deplete all the oxygen inside him. "I decided to take her to all the places she didn't get to go."

She placed her hand on his arm again, as much to tether herself to him as to aid his suffering. "That's so sweet," she said. She smiled at the bag.

Caleb looked at them, his expression sour and stern, then asked, "When did you decide to take your trip?"

"What difference does that make?" she asked.

"Couple hours ago," the man said. He patted a side of the bag. "She hasn't been like this that long. Gonna start with the entire west coast."

"How about that? We're both on a second honeymoon, sort of," she said, her tempo accelerating with each word, as if she were afraid her allotted time to answer was about to expire. "The first one was less than romantic. Let's put it that way."

Her face grew warm and she felt her spirit trying to rise, as it had done so easily in the airport. But she felt stuck, grounded within the swelling warmth of her body. She turned to Caleb, as if she might need the barf bag. But then she saw the disdain in his expression. Of course, he took her remark as a slight against him.

She turned back to the stranger.

No one spoke. She thought she was sweating, like the stranger, and feared she might drown in the flood of her own fluids. But when she touched her forehead, her dry fingers slid across her skin.

"What happened to her?" she heard herself ask in a voice that didn't sound like her.

"Seriously?" Caleb whispered. "You need to trade me seats. Before this nut job attacks you."

"God did it," the stranger said, as if it were a matter of fact and not a subject of dispute.

"God doesn't kill," Caleb said too loudly.

"All right. It was the tornado."

His statement seemed to be heard by the entire plane. No one turned to look but the sounds of the passengers became hushed.

"This last one?" she asked. "Oh, no. It was bad. I'm so sorry."

"F5. Biggest hook echo ever documented. God's enforcer. He brought quite a set of power tools."

Caleb looked around, as if he still might need a flight attendant's aid.

"Must be so hard. We live in Daggs. Hour and a half southeast of the City. All we got were downed trees," she said as if she were apologizing.

"But we've been hit," Caleb said, as if everything was a competition. "A few years ago, one blew half a trailer park away. But no one died. We got them all to safety." She put a hand on his arm and tried to puncture his stupidity with her colorful nails. "I'm a pastor. Hey!" he said removing her hand as if it were a cat. "Given the eulogy at a lot of funerals. You see the grief. You hug it. You hear it. You see it. But you know you can't touch it. Only God can. Tornados aren't God. They come to steal our blessings but can't get them without destruction. That's not God. He doesn't want our blessings. That's why he gave them to us. He's not a thief in the night. This is a fallen world. Not the world God created. We have to live in the one we brought into being. Until we return home to Him. Then this world will seem like a strange dream we had as children, one we might not even remember."

Though the stranger was smiling, his face was stricken as he opened the bag, which was still in Lyndsie's lap, as if it wasn't grief that pained him but his sense of humor. It took him a moment to unwind the twist tie. He handed it to Caleb, who declined. He pointed it at her but her hands were on the bag so he tied it onto her ring finger, where it formed an awkward pair with her wedding ring. "Ashes to ashes indeed. I guess it's the white privilege in me, but I have to admit I thought she'd be more like ocean sand. Wouldn't you expect Barbie to be refined and soft? Smooth, little grains. All the same size. Like sand through the hourglass. All individual yet blending perfectly. Love to feel your hand in. Your arm. Your—"

"We get it!" Caleb said.

"But, look," he said, sticking a prong of fingers into the ashes, coming forth with a claw of contents he sprinkled into a cupped hand. As he presented the ashes, he separated them so they could all be seen individually but it looked as if he was a prospector sorting through river silt for a gold nugget.

The ashes were gray but not fine like powdered sugar. More like finely-crushed gravel. Rough and jagged as tiny teeth.

Caleb's chin turned tight and he became interested in the laminated evacuation plan in the seat pocket. He flipped the large card over and then flipped it back.

Lyndsie couldn't take her eyes off the ashes. "Are you

planning to…" she said, her voice turning into a diminishing tunnel. She was barely able to pronounce the word scatter.

He grinned, as if she were kidding, but in the next breath he looked as if she'd told him his tumor was inoperable. "No, I'm always gonna have her. I can never let her go."

"That's not her," Caleb said, as if he were reading step one of the evacuation plan.

"That's what I said! But they had her name on them and they handed them to me. I paid them and then walked out the door. Took me a long time in the parking lot. I couldn't decide where to put her for the ride home. Or if I needed to fasten the seatbelt." The stranger looked as if he might vomit, but tears not bile departed his body. His chin quivered, rattling the weird grin etched on his face. He removed the tie from his pocket and dabbed his tears and his nose.

He opened a hand that had become a fist. The ashes it held were tamped into his skin. He needed both hands so he scraped them gently into her open palm. She didn't want to touch them. She closed her hand around them, as if to put them away, but they scratched and stung.

"Father, we know this isn't Lindsey," Caleb said.

"Again with the praying," the man said. Lyndsie grinned.

"She is with you," Caleb continued. "In the care and comfort of your heavenly home. We hold onto things, Father. We know we're weak."

"I'd like to know what they talk about. She and God. Or do you start with Jesus or the Holy Ghost and work your way up to the big man?" Caleb tried to interrupt. Lyndsie kept staring at the ashes. "You have God's line tapped? Do they talk about food? Clothes? Interior design? The nature of evil? Or maybe she's just describing the terror of the kids."

"No, no. There is no more terror. They are there with Him. With her."

"Do they laugh about it? Do they tell God? Of course, He knows what happened. But does He act like He hasn't heard the news? Does He get like distraught? That wouldn't seem genuine. He's already had time to process. He probably doesn't care. And I don't mean that as a knock. He's got a lot to look after. But you wonder if He acts like He cares but really He only loves the you that gets to come in. The rest has to stay outside."

"I think you start trying to read the mind of God you're in trouble."

"Don't have a choice. He quit talking to us."

"Yet you know He is here. Just like you know your wife is here. And in time you will forget about the pain and the suffering. Just like they have."

"Why do you bring up those kids?" she asked. "Was your wife a teacher?"

"Her name is Lindsey. Don't tell me you've already forgotten. Yes, she was a teacher."

"At that school?"

"Yes, at that school!"

Her legs jerked as if a sound wave had struck the reflex in her knee. The sack of ashes leaned toward its side but before it fell or lost an ash, his hand found the mouth and hers the tail.

"Your love shows God is with you," she said. "That He exists." Caleb attempted to intercede but she continued. "With us. And when we all get back home, you're going to call me and we're going to build a shrine. Wreaths of photos of her and her students. All together in an unbroken circle."

"I'm not bringing her back."

"But you said—"

"I can be a bit impulsive. Does it show?" He tried to laugh but no sound came out. "You never know what I'm going to do. Just like God. Or a tornado. Or your wife. Who told you on the phone to turn around and go home. She was on her way. And you believed her when you knew she would stay until the last kid had left the building."

The only sound was the fabric of Caleb's jeans brushing the seat cushion as his leg rocked impulsively.

She hugged the bag more securely onto her lap. "The city should build a monument to her and those poor ki— those poor…children."

"I sent the city plans for a shrine. I thought a sculpture of a ceiling collapsing onto them because you don't have enough bus drivers to get all the kids to safety and your tornado shelter is an annex because it has one concrete wall because the voters in your school district voted down a school bond that would have required fallout shelters..."

"Everything got so angry and ugly in the run-up to that election," she said to Lindsey more than to the men beside her.

There was another silence.

Caleb's leg had stopped rocking. He was no longer asking for an attendant. The man at the window continued with the description of his proposal, which included a depiction of the kid who bled out and an eternal flame in the form of his wife's 911 call.

"She told you what she wanted you to know," she said, smoothing a wrinkle in the black velvet, sitting up straighter because the bag felt heavier.

"She had no regrets," Caleb said, surprising them. "Because she did what her spirit was called to do. Now I am going to say another prayer. But instead of roadblocking your brain at the prayer sign, listen for her spirit. Because, Lord, we know you are here. With us now. And we know she is here. As she was at the school on that awful day. We don't understand, Lord, this world, in spite of our science. We don't understand all of Your Ways. But we know we are of spirit. We know it did not come from the ground, from the mud, from a single cell, from our organs and bones. It came from You and we honor that and thank you because we know spirit is what gave this woman such amazing love and compassion and courage. A creature of flesh and blood would have fled. But her spirit was called and she answered that call and she is with us now as we honor it and accept that we too are spirit. For those who live according to the flesh set their minds on the things of the flesh, but those who live according to the spirit set their minds on the things of the spirit. To set the mind on the flesh is death, but to set the mind on the spirit is life and peace. Let this spiritual communion be her shrine. Let it comfort and keep us.

Though we walk through the valley of the shadow of death, we fear not. Because it is through spirit that we journey. And you are with us. Amen."

Echoes of his last word found their way to both ends of the plane.

When the captain announced they were beginning their approach to their first stop, the man came to life as if he'd just awakened from a long sleep. She shifted Lindsey into the cradle of her arm farthest from him.

"Anyone want something to eat?" he asked. "It's on me."

"I'm starving," Caleb said. "All we get are pretzels all the way to Seattle."

"That's where I'm going."

"We've got an hour."

"Which is three hours airport time."

"Ha! You know it. We can catch some of the Broncos' game. It'll be on every screen in the terminal."

"My fantasy team's in trouble. And I've got two Broncos starting."

"Mine, too! Maybe we can help each other out before the late games start."

He grabbed the duffel and slid toward the aisle before she had time to move her legs. He started to follow Caleb but stopped. He felt for his wallet. He looked in the duffel. Then he remembered.

"It's okay," she said, shifting Lindsey to the other arm.

"Gotta get some clothes," he said, showing the meager contents in his bag.

The twist tie that secured the bag was still tied to her wedding ring. She bound it a turn tighter and then touched the ashes. She caressed them and then worked her fingers gently until they were one with the ashes, spreading them as she did when she pointed them to the sky, as if only they could hear the echo of a distant song, one that required a different form of surrender.

"Is he gonna lose, Daddy?" Calvin asked. "I'm scared."

"Don't be scared!" Murl said. "Big boys don't get scared. He'll find a way."

Calvin sat cross-legged on the splotched wooden floor, staring at the set with his one visible eye. The other was shielded by masking tape, which covered the left lens of his wire-frame glasses. The lens had been broken for some time, but looking at it still made Murl want to punch the wall.

"Come on, Wonder Boy!" Calvin shouted. "Make your temple gun!"

He was a small, frail, sandy-haired boy with little round ears that stuck out, and a pug nose. He was seven years old but his size and features made him look like a preschooler. As he watched the match, he gasped, clenched his teeth, squeezed his interlocked hands.

Murl wished he wouldn't do those things. He was acting like a sissy. But at least he was showing an interest in a fighting hero.

"Pile drive that beer belly!" yelled Murl's mother, an old woman with a red bandanna on her head and long fingers that squirmed in her lap like a cluster of snakes. She sat on the edge of a rust-colored divan next to Murl's father, a thin, sallow man with wispy hair and whiskers, wearing a baby blue windbreaker. When she slapped the sagging cushion between them, dust motes rose thick as gnats in the rays of sunlight that shot through holes in the faded orange pull-down blinds behind her. "If Wonder Boy loses, ain't gonna count. That River Rat's the sorriest scum ever set two feet in a ring!"

The Headleys watched as the River Rat, a large bearded man in cut-off overalls, pummeled the Wonder Boy, who was being held against a turnbuckle by a cheating River Rat brother while another distracted the referee in the far corner by pretending he was an FBI agent.

The Boy was a sight to be pitied. A lean, muscular blond man, clad in red, white, and blue trunks, and silver shoes with gold tassels, he slumped in the corner, arms draped across the ropes like a torture victim.

The Wonder Boy was wrestling's new all-American hero. He was so good it was hard for Murl to believe he was a real wrestler. He never screamed or hollered at his opponent before the match, never ranted or raved. He knew all the moves and holds, but never made the other wrestler suffer, no matter how evil he was. The Wonder Boy didn't cheat or scheme, back break, pile drive or eye gouge. He had a special weapon, but rarely used it. Most times Murl couldn't remember how he won the match. His opponents lunged, grabbed, thrashed, fumed, whined, cursed, and lost.

The Wonder Boy was so honorable he made Murl suspicious, but he didn't question the Boy's motives or actions aloud because his son had taken an interest. Calvin never watched wrestling until the Wonder Boy appeared on the scene. The other wrestlers scared and confused him, but the Wonder Boy made him feel safe and strong. More than once, Murl had seen Calvin clench his fist or stomp the floor as the Wonder Boy hurled his opponent into the ropes or flipped him to the mat. Calvin saw his first Wonder Boy match a week after the fight that broke his glasses. He hadn't missed one since. Neither had Murl. His son needed help from somewhere.

The Wonder Boy was in a fix this time, though. The River Rat was no fat-faced, dimple-cheeked cream puff. He had more tricks than a cat had hair, and had made more than one golden good guy beg for mercy with his vice-grip choke-hold. He taunted the Boy, then paraded around the ring, arms raised in victory, to the dismay of the crowd, except the few who cheered their bad guy hero. A broad hand cupping his ear, he leaned against the ropes, his back to the Wonder Boy, and motioned for the crowd to boo louder.

"Call your dogs now," Murl's father said. He sucked his teeth in dismay.

"Oh, no!" Calvin said. He tensed, shoulders shaking.

"It's all right," Murl said, too loudly. His voice frightened Calvin.

"Hush!" Murl's mother said, slapping the divan again. "Murl, where's Wanita? Wonder Boy needs all our support."

"In bed. Resting."

"Hmm!" she snorted. The old woman clasped her hands together, closed her eyes, and said a silent prayer. She liked the Wonder Boy almost as much as Calvin, because she said he was the only humble, God-fearing fighter on TV. When she opened her eyes, her face brightened at the sight on the screen. "Look!" she shouted.

While the Rat mocked the crowd, the Wonder Boy fell from the ropes to the canvas floor. On bent knees, he lifted his eyes toward the ceiling. He had a funny look on his face, as if he were listening to someone. A moment later, his face calm and serene, he raised his interlocked hands above his head. When he pointed his index fingers skyward, the crowd roared. The undisguised brother, who had been holding the Wonder Boy, fell to the floor, unconscious.

The FBI River Rat brother, who was still talking to the referee, spotted the Boy before the Rat did, and backpedaled into the turnbuckle, trembling. Scrambling, he opened his briefcase, which contained stacks of bills, and offered them to the Wonder Boy. Smiling, the Boy refused. The FBI River Rat brother closed the briefcase, climbed through the ropes and fled the arena. The River Rats were ignorant country hicks, but they knew enough to fear the temple gun, a respect the Wonder Boy's sophisticated foes needed more than one lesson to learn.

The Rat turned to see his brother in retreat. He stomped his foot in disgust, but when he saw the Boy standing with his aimed temple gun, he shook with fear. No one, including the Wonder Boy, could predict the gun's effects. Once, it gave the Exterminator amnesia for two months. In a single night, it flipped the Butcher Block out of the ring, and made Toxic Waste cluck like a chicken. Sometimes, nothing happened.

The Wonder Boy closed his eyes and fired. The lights in the arena went out.

"Hey!" Murl cried. "Pa, you on the remote?"

"Am not! Sitting by your mother."

"No remote control turned out them lights!" Murl's mother yelled.

When the lights returned, the Rat was on his knees, begging for mercy. As he cowered in fear, the Boy picked him up by his ear, and led him around the ring to the crowd's delight. The Wonder Boy was good and fair, but was no lace-on-his-britches sissy boy. He punched the Rat's bearded face, then kneed his hairy gut.

Refusing to pummel him the way another wrestler would, his control made the crowd scream that much louder. He finally calmed his fans with a patient hand, then raised his arm above his head. After a long moment of silence, he gave the Rat a swift chop to the neck. The Rat fell to the floor. The Wonder Boy pinned him with one hand.

"Glorious!" Murl's mother declared.

"Yeah!" Calvin shouted, jumping up and down. "He won, Daddy, he won!"

"You knew he'd pull it out," Murl said, relieved. The last thing Calvin needed to see was a Wonder Boy loss. Murl was always amazed when the Wonder Boy won a match, and knew the temple gun was just a gimmick. But if the Boy could help Calvin, Murl was for him, even if he was a borderline sissy. Murl slid out of his chair and onto the floor where he began pushing Calvin, hoping to goad him into wrestling with him.

"What you get messing with the Wonder Boy, you bottom-dwelling, silt-sucking river scum!" Murl's mother said. "Three River Rats ain't no match for the Wonder Boy and his Lord."

"That's what I should have done to them guys broke my glasses," Calvin said, aiming his temple gun at the set.

"You'll handle them prissy-whipped pansies next time," Murl said, bending Calvin's ear back until he said ouch. "But remember, the temple gun only works for the Wonder Boy."

"Memaw said it can work for anyone."

"Well yeah but—"

"'Murl Headley, what are you telling that boy?" his mother cried. Her words were so strong they seemed to make the black visqueen that covered the large broken front window behind the TV bristle and pop.

"Nothing!" Murl claimed. The woman had better ears than a German Shepherd. Watham's snoring next door could keep her up at night.

"You ain't telling him them lights went out cause of a power failure, are ya?"

"No but—"

"I cursed the day I saw you had brains. I told Pa, some day that boy'll lose faith cause he'll think he can take care of everything hisself. Surprised you ain't rooting for the River Rat or that evil serpent, Reverend Death, by now."

"I ain't telling Calvin nothing bad, Mama. But next time he gets jumped by them panty-assed rich kids, I don't want him standing there with his fingers pointed while they beat the piss out of him."

"Watch your mouth, Murl Headley. I'm not too old to lather your tongue."

"Sorry, Mama." Murl lowered his head.

"Gonna take more than the Wonder Boy and a temple gun to get this'n to take up for himself," his mother continued. "You can twist his ears till they come off, and he won't do nothing but cry. Wanita's turned you both into babies."

"Murl?" a voice called.

"Here we go," Murl's mother said.

"What?" Murl bellowed.

"Can you come here?"

"What for?"

"Because I'm pregnant with your second child, that's what for!"

"All right!"

"Mommy still sick?" Calvin asked.

"She's just resting."

"Murl?"

"I'm coming!"

Murl walked down the hall to the first bedroom, which he shared with Wanita and Calvin. His parents slept in the other bedroom at the end of the hall. They moved in about a year ago after the house they had lived in for nineteen years burned to the ground from an overloaded light socket. Murl was glad to help them out. He never had liked living twenty-five miles from his mama. But he had to admit their presence had added to his troubles. The landlord raised the rent twenty-five dollars, and Wanita and Murl's mother had been at odds from day one.

The paneled bedroom was too small for three people. From the door, you could barely see the tiny mattress where Calvin slept. It lay on the floor near Murl and Wanita's full-size bed. A pale woman with dirty blonde hair that was as limp as her body lay on the bed, an open box of Little Debbie Swiss Cakes and a paperback novel, *Blind Passion*, beside her. A purple blanket covered her, even though the temperature had reached eighty degrees earlier that afternoon. She looked up at Murl with odd but stunning sky-blue eyes that had always entranced him.

"How you feeling, darling?"

"I'm not dying, you know. Can't tell your mother that."

"Don't worry about her."

"It's just in the mornings, Murl. But it makes me so tired."

"It's all right. Whatever you need to do is fine."

"Your mama thinks it's all in my head. She said she never felt better in her whole life than when she was carrying you. Sang like a meadowlark all day long. She don't sing that good, Murl."

"I'll talk to her."

"I don't think she wants me to have it."

"Wanita."

"Do you?"

"Yes, sweetheart. You know that."

"Still think I'm pretty?"

"Course I do."

"Murl!" his mother called. "Someone at the door."

Murl sighed, then felt the frustration join the pit of rage that seemed to be replacing his stomach. "Crying out loud," he muttered. "Can't things come to a stop for one minute?"

"Don't answer it. Stay in here with me and snuggle."

"Murl!"

"All right! Guess I'm the only one in the house who can turn a door knob."

Murl's black boots, which had scuffed toes and red diamonds on the side, made a heavy, thudding noise on the wooden floor as he stomped across the living room. He brushed back his dark, oily hair, and pulled down his black Batman t-shirt, which looked a size too small, before opening the door.

When he did, he was surprised by the sight, even though he knew the woman standing on the narrow porch. It was Jerri Taylor, their Child Welfare worker. Murl got along all right with Jerri, but he knew why she was there, and had to check an impulse to slam the door in her chubby face.

"Murl, I need to see Calvin." Normally a pleasant woman, her voice was as heavy as a rock. Murl stepped aside as she walked in.

"Well, looky here," Murl's mother said when she saw the woman. "Pa, better go make sure Calvin's underwear is in the right drawer."

"Mama, don't start it," Murl said. His mother hated anyone who worked for the government, even Jerri, who changed Murl's opinion of Child Welfare, and whom Calvin liked more than his teacher. Murl's mother said they sent a nice person out to hide their evil intentions. Anyone who watched the River Rat should know that trick.

"Hello, Mrs. Headley," Jerri said. "You're looking well."

Jerri never lost control of herself. She could dodge an insult as well as the Wonder Boy dodged punches, which impressed Murl. Before he met her, he always thought mild-mannered people were weak. He learned better the first time she came out to help them remove what the investigator called health and safety hazards. Murl had learned to control his temper, but the thought of a stranger invading his home frightened him. Encouraged by his mother's urging, he asked Jerri what she would do if he threw her roly-poly butt out the door. Without a second's thought, she told him if he was that strong he ought to be an Olympic weight lifter. It left Murl and his mama speechless. Then Jerri asked Calvin if he knew what a roly-poly was, and took him outside to show him one.

"Jerri!" Calvin said, running to her.

"Hello there, Captain Calvin. How's my favorite pirate?"

"Fine. Matey."

"And you're worried about this one," Jerri asked Murl.

"The other kids laugh when I go, 'Arrrgh. I'm Captain Calvin'."

"Guess they don't cover getting made fun of in her textbook," Murl's mother said. Murl looked at Jerri and grinned.

"They do cover it. Would you like to do some reading tonight?"

"No, ma'am, I don't. Be happy to write a chapter or two. Step one. Make a fist."

"Not many kids get to wear an eye patch, do they, Calvin?" Jerri looked at Murl but she wasn't grinning. "Calvin, can you see all right?"

"Sure."

"Ever get headaches at school?"

"No. Tommy Yost flicks my ears. That hurts."

"Do you tell the teacher?" Calvin shrugged his shoulders. "I brought you a surprise." She pulled a red lollypop from her pants pocket.

"Hey! Thank you!"

"After I'm gone, ask your dad and mom before you eat it. Okay? Don't want to spoil your supper."

"All right. Can I eat it now, Daddy?"

"Yeah, go ahead."

Jerri smiled at Calvin, then looked at Murl. "Can we talk?"

"Step two. Don't give out rewards less their deserved," Murl's mother said.

***

They walked into the kitchen, a long, dank room with dingy yellow cabinets and dirty dishes piled in the sink. The white paint on the plaster walls was badly flaked and chipped, leaving large beige spots. The tan and green linoleum flooring was curling up in the corners.

Murl moved an open black garbage bag, full of aluminum cans, so Jerri could sit down at the table. Her large thighs, clad in loose purple pants, flattened when she sat, spilling over both sides of the old wooden chair. Her dark eyes looked like teddy bear eyes pressed deep into her fleshy face. She was so good-natured, a trace of a smile lingered on her face even when she was upset. "What is going on, Murl? This is the third time I've been out about the glasses."

"I'm gonna take care of it. Soon as I get paid."

"You've been telling me that for two months."

Murl shrugged. "I know. I got a lot of bills."

"I believed you when you told me about the car."

"It's true. Go ask Jerald down at the Apco. Guess I shoulda made the guy who sold me that piece of junk pay."

"I don't want to interrogate you, but I'm getting suspicious. What else could be more important than Calvin's glasses?"

"Just stuff. The car, washing machine."

"That's hardly more important than Calvin's eyesight."

"Gotta have the car to go to work. If I don't work, I don't get paid and nobody gets nothing."

"You still won't apply for a medical card?"

Murl shook his head. "Don't need any handouts."

"There's no shame in it, Murl. That's what the program is for. You let Wanita do it for the pregnancy."

"Didn't have a choice. Not after they told me how much it was gonna cost. Can't even have a damn baby without getting robbed."

"The bills don't go away after they're born."

"Those people ask questions I wouldn't ask my own mother. And then they want to track your every step."

"I know it seems personal. But you can't support a family

this large making ten dollars an hour. You're doing all you can."

"Mama and Daddy been bringing in some."

"I'm not even going to ask."

"We can handle our own problems."

"Well, like it or not, this is my problem too. I'm not trying to be mean, you know that. But if you aren't going to fix Calvin's glasses, I'll pick him up at school and take him to Dr. Edwards myself, and have him send you the bill."

Murl's black boot began tapping the floor. "Don't do that, Jerri."

"I don't want to."

"Then don't. It's that damn school's fault."

"Mrs. Bridges is not to blame. She's just concerned about Calvin. She says he can't read in the afternoons because his eye gets tired."

"If they're so damned concerned, why didn't they do anything to the four kids who beat him up?"

"Mr. Baldwin told me personally it was only one and he's been disciplined. We've been over this. Now it's up to you to fix Calvin's glasses."

"All right!" Murl snapped. He stirred in his chair. "I get paid on the first."

"How are things at work?"

"We're gonna do the grounds for that new hospital. Might get some overtime."

"Good. Wanita okay?"

"Yeah. Just sick a lot."

Jerri nodded. "I know things are tough. Want me to make the appointment with Dr. Edwards?"

"No."

"All right. I'm sorry, Murl. But you've got to fix those glasses soon as you get paid."

Before she left, Jerri stopped and talked with Calvin, who was playing with a GI Joe that had a missing right arm. After she was gone, Murl stared at the pockmarked door, then beat and kicked it, twice. He tromped into the kitchen, to get away from the door, and hurled the garbage bag against the wall, slinging bent, dripping cans clanking across the floor.

He slurped a big drink of water from the faucet. He wasn't sure why he was so mad, but he did know why he hadn't fixed Calvin's glasses. Until that boy got revenge and learned to take up for himself, he would look at the world with one eye.

***

Murl heard a god-awful scream. He rushed into the living room to find his mother bent down in front of the television, fingers flapping at her sides, mouth open, eyes wild as a trapped cat. "Looky, Murl. Look at the screen and tell me Pa ain't lying."

"She don't believe nothing I say," Murl's father said, sucking his teeth. "Never has, never will."

On the set, Murl saw the masked face of Reverend Death who wore a priest's collar but had a skull and crossbones instead of a cross around his neck. He was staring into the camera as he berated the Wonder Boy. It took Murl a second to catch the message running across the bottom of the screen, announcing the future pairing of Reverend Death and the Wonder Boy—two foes who had yet to meet in the ring—at several specially selected sites, including Oklahoma City's Myriad on May fifth.

"Is it true?" Murl's mother asked, her voice timid with hope.

He almost lied so he wouldn't have to hear the scream of joy that was about to erupt. "It's true," Murl said.

"Are we going, Daddy?" Calvin asked after he quit holding his ears, looking at Murl with his one visible eye. "Please?" The TV cut to the Wonder Boy, who was standing outside the ring, signing autographs for kids.

"Of course, we are!" Murl's mother replied. Taking Calvin's hands, she danced in circles with him, singing, "Going to see the Wonder Boy! Going to see the Wonder Boy!"

That night as Murl lay in bed, he looked at Calvin while Wanita read an Isaac Asimov novel to him. They didn't own many children's books, and Wanita's science fiction stories confused and bored Murl, but Calvin didn't complain. He liked the strange worlds in the books, which she kept stacked neatly in a corner of the room with her romance novels. Calvin's toys huddled in the other corner.

Wanita was the smart one, not Murl. She could have gone to college. She told Calvin that Isaac Asimov was America's greatest writer. She also told him that with his daddy's energy and her intelligence, he had as good a chance as anyone to be somebody.

Murl looked at Calvin's sandy hair, the freckles on his cheeks and forearms, the curve of his elbow and knee, his little hands. He looked just like Wanita, which made Murl proud and afraid. Murl loved his son, but he couldn't stand to see him weak and frightened. He wanted to toughen Calvin up, but every time he tried he scared the boy, making him even more scared. Helping him was like trying to catch water with your hands.

The thought of other boys picking on Calvin made Murl angry enough to pull bricks out of a wall. Calvin got picked on some during first grade, but it stopped after a while. This year, it hadn't stopped. After the fight that broke Calvin's glasses, Murl didn't taunt him, wrestle with him, slap him in the face to get him to punch back, or even talk with him. Nothing had worked, so he said, "When you get the boy back that broke your glasses, I'll fix 'em. Not until."

Like everything else he tried on Calvin, this plan backfired. He expected Calvin to lie, and was prepared to check his story, walking right into the boy's classroom and asking the other kid, if he had to. But Calvin didn't start a fight with the boy or claim he had. When Murl asked him about it, every day after school for three weeks, Calvin shrugged his shoulders or said he didn't get a chance or cried or asked why people hurt one another.

Lying in bed, Murl remembered a time when he was a boy,

growing up in Levi, a tiny country town twenty-five miles north of Daggs. He was standing in a neighbor's yard, watching the owner of the house burn a pile of leaves. A group of kids had gathered, and one of them, ten-year-old Junior Starks, grabbed Murl's Indian headdress and threw it on the fire. Murl watched it burn to nothing as everyone laughed. He pushed Junior, yelling, then ran home bawling.

His father was lying on the divan, as usual, doing nothing. After his mother calmed Murl and heard the story, she got hotter than the fire. Grabbing a belt, she headed for the door.

"Eunice!" Murl's father shouted. "You gonna fight all the boy's battles for him? Make him go kick that boy's ass."

She stopped, swatted the door with the belt. "Your daddy's right. You go fight that boy or you don't eat tonight." Murl didn't respond. "You hear me?" She cuffed him on the side of the head with her wrist, then slapped his other cheek.

That was the first time he felt the rage. This was different from getting mad. It was like the shame turned everything inside him to liquid and the anger set it to boiling, pressing the wall of his stomach, then his chest, arms, neck, head. She hit him again, hard. He took a swing at her. "Not me, tater head! Him!" Murl followed the direction of her point, storming out the front door. "I'll be watching from the window," he heard her say as he tromped up the street. Murl was eight years old.

As if he were being pushed by tornado air, Murl walked right up to the jeering Junior Starks and punched him in the chest. The boys grappled for a while before Junior took him to the ground, pinning Murl's arms with his knees, punching him in the chest and taunting him. Murl caught his breath, then found a reserve of strength in his panic, and knocked Junior off-balance enough so he could roll out from under him. He scrambled to his feet, turned, and kicked. His foot caught Junior in the groin, making him curl up like a whipped pup. Murl kicked him three more times before the other boys scattered at the sight of an approaching car. Murl ran home where his mother hugged him and took him to the Big Blue for an ice cream cone. After that day, Junior made fun of other kids, and tried to get little Murl, as he called him, to laugh with him.

In high school, no one wanted to mess with Murl Headley. Other kids made fun of him, but never to his face. His anger helped him, but his fists were the only thing he had to oppose someone with. Getting into fights cost him three jobs after high school. Sometimes, when he was in a bad mood, a smart-ass comment or a look would set him off, and he'd fly into the guy.

He didn't see the need to handle himself better until he nearly lost Wanita. She was the sweetest, prettiest woman he'd ever met. She liked him, said brains and brawn rarely came in the same package. But during their second fight, Murl pushed her down so hard a knot formed on the back of her head after she hit the wall. She told him that was strike one, two, and three.

He begged her for two weeks to give him another chance. He brought her a new romance novel every day. When she wouldn't accept it, he plopped down in the yard near her bedroom window and read it aloud. One day, he brought a science fiction novel. She walked onto the porch, listened to him try to read it. He didn't read very well. After a few minutes, she sat down beside him and read the first chapter.

"Mama's gotta go pee. Again," Wanita said to Calvin. "I'll finish when I get back."

"You like that story?" Murl asked.

"Yeah. Mama reads good."

"She sure does."

"We gonna see the Wonder Boy?"

Murl took a deep breath. "I don't know."

"We're not?"

"We'll see. You like the Wonder Boy, don't you?"

"Yeah. He's never afraid."

"You're tough, too." Murl touched Calvin's tender biceps with a thick, rough hand. The skin was so different you wouldn't think they were the same kind of creature. Murl's fingernails, which were cut short, looked as if they had been mashed with a vise into the flesh. The one on his index finger was only half-grown, the skin below it black and purple. Calvin's skin was as smooth as a ripe banana. "And you're big and strong, like the Wonder Boy."

"No, I'm not," Calvin said, giggling. "The Wonder Boy's big, like you."

"You're gonna be big and strong."

"When I'm ten years old I will be."

"You can't wait that long. When someone grabs you, you need to—"

"Oww," Calvin said, touching Murl's hand. He was squeezing Calvin's arm.

***

Murl decided that seeing the Wonder Boy in person was his last hope for helping Calvin learn to fight. The only problem was he couldn't take the family to see the Wonder Boy and fix Calvin's glasses in the same month. And he knew Jerri would check on Calvin again before the end of the month.

Murl thought for three days before he came up with a plan. He drove to Walmart, Wall's, the Dollar General and Dollar Tree and Family Dollar, even Goodwill and the Salvation Army store in search of a pair of glasses that would fit Calvin. But he had no luck.

Then he thought of Watham, his neighbor. Watham liked to read hot rod and soldier of fortune magazines and kept a drawer full of store-bought glasses. Murl told Watham he wanted to borrow a pair so he could do his own test of Calvin's eyesight. He said he didn't trust Calvin's eye doctor. While Murl searched the drawer, Watham, who was examining a new Chinese assault rifle he bought mail order, explained to him why he shouldn't trust any doctor. Most of the frames were too large, but at the bottom of the drawer lay a pair of small, round tortoise shell frames. Normally, Murl would never let Calvin wear such a pair. He would really look like a bookworm sissy in them. But they would fit.

The best part of Murl's plan was his element of surprise.

Instead of waiting on Jerri to drop in and check on Calvin, he decided to call her and invite her over for an inspection before the day of the Wonder Boy match. That would throw her suspicions off, allowing them to see the Wonder Boy and giving Murl until the first of the month to fix the glasses.

The night before Jerri's scheduled visit, Murl called the family into the living room, except Calvin, and explained the plan. Jerri was coming to the house at 5:30. Murl would meet her in the yard and tell her they were heading to the park. Murl's mother and father would be in the back seat of the car, Calvin between them when Jerri pulled up. This way Jerri wouldn't get too close to the boy, and wouldn't stay as long. After he spoke with Jerri, Murl would call Wanita out of the house. They would get into the car and drive off.

"That government woman's turned you into the River Rat, Murl Headley," his mother huffed. "I ain't gonna be part of no scheme. We'll tell her we ain't fixing the glasses til we want to, and nuts to her if she don't like it."

"Mama, this is the only way we can go see the Wonder Boy without making Jerri mad. She can take Calvin away if she decides to, whether you like it or not. If you won't go along with the plan, then you just won't go see the Wonder Boy."

"You'll go without me over my dead body!" she proclaimed. A long finger pointed toward a spot near the front door, about where the dead body would be.

"Why do we even need to go to the Wonder Boy?" Wanita asked.

Murl's mother cocked her head, raised her eyebrows, and glared at Murl. "How many times am I gonna have to say it? How long is it gonna take you to figure out—"

"That you ain't nothin' but an old guinea hen who clucks all day and treats her son like he was still in diapers."

"Guinea hen? Now!" Murl's mother said, her right hand slapping at the air in front of her as if she were trying to hit Wanita's words. "Pregnant don't mean I'm about to stand here and take lip off some prissified Maybelline."

"Enough! Both of ya! I'm runnin' this family and I'll say

what goes. And if you two don't like it I'll knock down ever wall in this house and you can both sleep outside."

"Pay him mind," Murl's father said. "He's gotten awful strong framing walls and knows where their weak points are."

***

The next day Murl made himself throw up, so he could show J.D. his boss he was sick and get off an hour early. When he got home, his wallet stuffed with bills from his cashed paycheck, his parents were still out hunting cans so they could buy an autographed Wonder Boy photo for their wall. Wanita was asleep and Calvin was playing in the living room. Murl sat down but didn't turn the television on. He thought through the plan again to see if he could find any hidden glitches.

He looked over at Calvin. The boy always had an assortment of stuff on that side of the room, but Murl never paid much attention to it. Calvin had placed two rusty, worn-out lawn chairs, backs facing, about eight feet apart, connecting them with two strands of loose string. On the string he had placed twigs, popsicle sticks, and cut drinking straws, forming a long, imitation rope bridge. String with tiny knots tied in it hung down the sides of both chairs. Under the bridge were two boats hand-fashioned out of newspaper and three small dinosaur figures made from Play-Doh.

"Calvin," Murl said loudly, for no reason other than he was surprised by what he saw.

"I'm sorry, Daddy," Calvin said, dropping the object in his hand, which clanked on the floor. His head drooped and he turned his shoulders away as Murl approached. "I know I'm not supposed to use a can for a toy."

Murl looked at the floor. Two cans with holes punched in the bottoms were connected by a stick. "What are you doing with this?"

Calvin trembled. "Trying to make a car."

Murl gazed at the elaborate bridge construction. "You made all this?"

"Yeah, I'll take it down. I'll find Memaw some more cans to make up for these."

"No, it's all right," Murl said, placing his hand on Calvin's shoulder. "How were you going to make a car out of these cans?"

"I'm sorry. I know I wasn't supposed to—"

"It's okay. Show me."

"Well, see, they'll roll like this," he said, demonstrating. "But when I hook them to another one, I can't make it work."

"It's a good start. This stick is what you call an axle on a car. You put the wheels on the ends of it, just like you did, and that makes the wheels turn. You have one for the front wheels and one for the back."

"How do you hook them together?"

"You have to make a frame with holes in it for the axle to fit through. We could do it, but I'll have to think for a while to figure out what to use."

Murl looked closely at the bridge. He touched it, noticing the planks didn't shift. "You glue these on?"

"Yeah."

"Today?"

"No. I keep that in the back yard."

"This took a lot of work, Calvin."

"Thanks, Dad. Mom helped me with it. We're making my own world like those she reads about in space."

Murl had the strangest feeling of his life. It seemed like he was watching Wanita as a young kid play but it was Calvin, his son. He noticed the masking tape on Calvin's glasses. It looked like a big scab covering one of his blue eyes. A problem Murl knew how to fix.

"Come on," he said, standing.

"Where we going?"

"To the eye doctor."

A Coke and a Cigarette

I knew I was going to kill him. That ain't what got me, I don't care what you or Dumbass the Detective think. A narc is a nothing, what I say.

His name was Lance Shipley. I didn't know the man. I don't live here. I'm from McClanahan County, where a man knows what to expect if he rolls on another man. People here are civilized, which means they don't object to making deals with the law when they get caught breaking it.

My cousin, Jerrod Darter, called me two weeks ago. He was scared. He'd been bouncing around for a couple of years, finally got himself pinched. He was a fuck-up, I'll admit, even though he's blood. Not because he got stoned, laid around, didn't like to work. But because he did these things and still dreamed of something else. I'd hand him the joint, talking of quail or coyotes or budding plants or wood, and he'd lean against the house, his brown eyes slick and flat as bottle caps, nodding not to words but to sounds. Whatever was floating in his head seemed like smoke to me. Eventually, it filled his mind. He couldn't see or breathe. So he ran.

As long as he stayed on the road, he kept his head clear, or so it seemed. He went from Hugo to Paris, Texas, to Daggs to Ardmore, where he stayed a while, to Duncan, back to Ardmore, then down to the place of big dreams, big smoke, Dallas, Texas. There, he found out what it was really like to be trapped. He went junkie for a time, shooting crank so he could feel like he was going somewhere as he crawled up the overpass he called home. Dallas didn't swallow him. Jerrod must have had enough damp soil and sticky leaves in his blood to work against the junk and the concrete.

He bounced up to Otto of all places, a clean, rigid, Baptist town. He laid carpet, met a girl, attended church. None of the three took.

There's money in Otto, which is another reason I hate the place. Money and drugs, scraps and raccoons. They find each other. Even in a town with a curfew for teenagers, a Walmart

Super Center, and refurbished Main Street storefronts. People don't know how steady the flow is, how quickly cash can build a pipeline. They think one more big push, planes above the border with orders to shoot, boots on the ground led by dogs, choppers and searchlights raiding the highways and the fields. They just don't know. Might as well declare war on ticks.

So Jerrod called, sounding like he was talking with his bones. This dude, Lance Shipley, was ratting people out. He'd worn a wire for the cops after they stopped him driving home from the bar, drunk, and found his stash, a dozen quarter-bags of crank. Enough to put him away. He rolled on his supplier— the righteous thing to do in Otto—then got a kick out of the power and attention, and kept narcing. Jerrod said he was still snorting to show he wasn't a rat. And the cops knew. He was playing both sides.

I give him credit. He must have had some smarts. But a narc is a nothing. He ain't a witness who saw some old lady get raped or a kid get punched out by his stepfather. He ain't a cop but to them he ain't a criminal either. He's a nothing, and this nothing was going to send my cousin away.

Jerrod had trusted him. The smoky-headed ones always believe in strangers. Lance was cool, Jerrod thought. Now Jerrod was sure Mr. Cool had him on tape, selling, but Jerrod was convinced the cops were laying low, hoping for a big round-up bust. Local elections were three months away. Jerrod figured they wanted one more score before word got out on Lance Shipley. Fear is a good thing sometimes; it was blowing the smoke out of Jerrod's head like a cold winter wind.

I told Jerrod he was a fuck-up. He agreed. He said he didn't want to go to jail. Without the testimony of Lance Shipley, the tape was worthless. I asked about Shipley's family. They would determine how hard the police would work to solve his murder. Jerrod said Shipley had no contact with his father, who lived in Arizona; his mother, married four times, died two years ago of cancer. Shipley lived in a rent house. I told Jerrod I would take care of it.

There ain't no trick to murder, no matter who's wearing

guns. I could have kidnapped him, then done it way up in the Ouachita Mountains, but McClanahan County is a three-hour drive from Otto by highway. Too far to go with a body, and I couldn't account for some other unseen risks. And Lance Shipley was in regular contact with local cops.

So I went to the one place where a narc ain't watched. His home.

Jerrod had done the surveillance. I knew then he was going to turn out all right. Lance Shipley could be found at his rent house on Rennie Street most mornings until 10:30 or 11:00. I was going to arrive at 9:30.

Friday night, my buddy Allen Gash and I went camping in the mountains. At three in the morning, we filled a thermos with coffee, loaded our jugs and trotlines, and pulled out, leaving our tent pitched, a low fire burning.

We went north, as a precaution, and drove into town as if we were coming down from Shawnee. Allen dropped me off in the Burger King parking lot where Jerrod's blue Grand Prix was parked. Jerrod was sitting in a booth, glancing out the plexiglass wall, sipping coffee. I walked into the bathroom and waited.

He looked the same but his eyes were different. The light was coming out instead of pouring in.

"Here's a map showing how to get there," he said, handing me a folded piece of paper he dropped once. Then he pulled a small envelope from his front pocket. "And here's something. It's not enough but I'll get you more when I can."

Inside the envelope was a wad of twenties. "I ain't of them," I said. I shoved his hand away, then grabbed the envelope and pulled out a single bill. "Gas money."

He started to leave, then stopped. "I don't know what to say. I can't go to jail. Just thinking about it..."

"Then stop thinking. The cops are going to come see you and everyone on that tape soon as they find his body. It's okay to be scared. Just don't tell them anything, no matter what threats they make. Without Lance Shipley, they won't be able to touch you."

He took a deep breath. "Thought about taking off but decided it would be less suspicious if I act like a fucked-up stoner who don't know nothing."

"You're a nothing to them. So just be yourself."

He didn't laugh. I told him to count to 200 before he left the bathroom then order food and eat every crumb. Then order ice cream and ask for a job application. Sit down, fill it out, and turn it in.

It was a fifteen-minute walk to Lance Shipley's. I passed two Baptist churches. Jerrod had told me there were more churches in town than convenience stores, which was saying something. I thought about narcs and Baptists and cops and people who liked telling other people what to do in the name of righteousness. It got me worked up.

Lance Shipley lived at 714 South Rennie in a red brick house with white shutters that had star-shaped holes in them and two white wrought-iron supports on the small concrete porch. The neighborhood was quiet, a mix of factory workers and old people. A metallic blue Dodge ram pickup gleamed in the narrow driveway. There wasn't a scratch on it. Seeing it made me think of Lance Shipley chamoising it with twenty-dollar bills.

The old .38 revolver went heavy inside my boot as I stepped onto the porch. I was no hit man. My heart throbbed. But I thought of Jerrod and turned the door knob. It was unlocked.

The front room was a place only a nothing would like. A big divan with palm trees in the fabric stood against one wall facing a plywood entertainment center that held a shiny television and a new stereo. On the wall were black-framed prints of that stylish, brunette cartoon-woman that appears in *Playboy*. Shipley was cool, all right.

For a moment I forgot why I was there. Then I heard the sound of a hair dryer. I took out the gun and tucked myself behind a kitchen wall beneath a neon Bud sign that wasn't plugged in. I looked at the back yard through the sliding glass door. I could see a mimosa tree beside the chainlink fence. A gravel alley separated the yard from the neighbors. There was no dog.

I went to my knees to lower my sightline. I stared at nothing, thought of the TV, the stereo, the framed prints, the Dodge truck, the gun in my hand.

When I heard steps, my hand flinched, and I nearly fired a nervous shot. A man walked into the kitchen, his back to me, and opened the refrigerator. It was Lance Shipley, looking just like Jerrod's description. He was wearing a striped denim shirt, new Wranglers, and ostrich-skin boots. His brown mullet was combed and wavy, still damp with gel.

When he turned around, I noticed a cigarette in the hand that popped the tab on a Coke. I wanted a Coke and a cigarette.

He took a drink and two steps before he saw me. His walking made me stand up. He started to speak but saw the gun. His mouth opened in surprise. That's where I shot him.

He fell straight back. I kept my feet from running. I wasn't going to escape in a chase. I didn't think the neighbors would call at the sound of one gunshot, especially at mid-morning. People can't believe it makes such a simple sound. I planned to wait fifteen minutes, wipe the door knob clean, then pull away slowly in Shipley's own truck.

I wasn't afraid to look at the dead Lance Shipley. I knew even a dead nothing would be an ugly sight. I decided to kill him and I had. His eyes were open, his mouth a nasty, red hole. None of that startled me.

What I saw next did.

The Coke and cigarette were still in his hands. Four fingers and a thumb gripped the full upright can. Not a drop had spilled. Smoke rose from the cigarette still wedged casually between an index and middle finger. I saw the cigarette glow as another ring on the paper burned away, joining the growing band of ashes.

A narc is a nothing, I told myself. I thought of the hidden tape, the bastard sitting smugly on the witness stand, my cousin behind bars, and I wanted to drill Shipley's skull with another slug. I tried not to but I looked at his hands again. They kept holding on.

I had told Allen Gash, many times, I wanted to die with a beer and a cigarette in my hands. I never imagined what that would look like. I felt thirsty. The Coke can was sweating, big watery drops sliding down the slick aluminum, one after the other.

I swear the can moved.

The first bullet pierced the can, which remained in Shipley's hand, then ripped into his thigh. The next one lifted his other hand off the floor. The cigarette landed on the blackened fingers. The third shot blasted through the man's cheek. I don't remember the other two.

The cops found the revolver on the kitchen floor. They caught me leaping over a trash dumpster in an alley several blocks away. I remember fighting, falling to the gravel. They hit me. One of them kicked me. I lay down in the back seat of the patrol car. They had to carry me into the county lock-up. Moron the Jailer asked if I was the new Scarface. His cheek still wears my teeth marks.

Jerrod had the guts to come see me, but he started crying, then yelling he was behind it all. I told Dumbass the Detective he was just a scared kid, that he didn't know nothing about nothing. I told him it was me on the tape. I told him Lance Shipley was a nothing.

"They're the hardest to kill," he said, shifting the toothpick in his clucking mouth.

"Wasn't too damned hard," I said.

"Mm-hmm."

He wanted me to take Shipley's place. There were people in my county they wanted. His belly pressed against his starched shirt. His striped tie couldn't hide the strain on the buttons. We sat there, waiting for one to pop. He didn't walk away until I flipped the table trying to grab one.

"If it weren't for you, he'd still be alive!" I yelled. "If it weren't for you, he wouldn't be a nothing!"

One Dalmatian

After work, Carmichael walked home, tapered shadow touching the steps a half block before he did. When he arrived, he stood on the porch, glancing back at his shadow, which leaned into the street, waiting for him to decide.

He tried to make something called dinner but he devoured half the ingredients during the preparation so he ate what was left standing over the sink.

"Speeds clean-up!" he thought to himself, which wouldn't have added to his concerns except he not only said it aloud, he shouted it, and then he not only shouted it, he fashioned a song and dance out of it.

After nightfall, Carmichael paced, pretending to dust and sweep and do his taxes. The TV and windows gave him back his reflection. He closed the blinds and clicked on the set.

There were a lot of channels but he struggled to settle on one. He flipped open his laptop. There were a lot of websites. He scrolled through the list of contacts on his phone. It took a while to read them all. When he was done, he called some of them with the phone on speaker while he changed channels with the remote and selected websites with the mouse.

He owned one rope. He had tied in one end a well-formed noose. He slipped the noose around his neck. He let the other end dangle. In this way he could sleep. But the rope rubbed his neck raw.

He wouldn't admit he was lonely. If he admitted he was lonely, he would have identified the problem. If he identified the problem, he would have to find a solution. The other end of the rope remained untied.

***

The next day he stood in line to see the guru/author DeLyte Ashram. Carmichael held no book but toted a grocery sack in his hands.

"Your words I have paid for and read," Carmichael said to

the man dressed in an Armani suit and cloak. "They are, like my life, fodder for the confetti of my spent celebrations. No words, not even a stylish autograph from you on the title page can help me."

Carmichael poured the torn pages of the book, *TV are Only Two Members of the Alphabet*, onto the floor.

"I respect your faith and your despair," DeLyte said, signaling the store manager, wiping the corner of his mouth with a monogrammed handkerchief.

Carmichael blew into the bag, preparation for popping.

"Did you watch Disney films as a boy?" DeLyte asked.

"Yeah, of course."

"Including *Pinocchio*?"

"Yes."

"You're not a real boy, are you?" Carmichael lowered the sack. "Get a dog."

"Huh?"

"You need a pet. Find a Dalmatian. The new movie is out. They will be plentiful."

"I'll name it Disney."

"Name it Disco. In honor of yourself. Loud, annoying, and poorly-dressed."

"Hey!"

"And only happy when in the presence of a mirror ball."

***

Even though Carmichael had bought the man's book, he didn't want to take his advice. But when he got home, a Dalmatian was sniffing his hedge.

It had a red collar and leash but no ID. Carmichael patted the dog's head, rubbed its floppy ears, stroked its back. It jumped on his chest, slobbering.

He opened the front door, told the dog to come in. She bolted into the neighbor's yard, chasing a falling leaf.

He called to her, then pursued her. She ran from him when

he came, then followed when he turned around. Finally, she cowered, groping the ground, tail thumping.

He ushered her into the house, told her to stay off the furniture.

She peed in the hall.

He escorted her to the back yard.

He nuzzled her, talked to her, tried to get her to sit, roll over, fetch a stick.

She did not want to leave his petting hand.

He had to push her back with his foot to close the door.

He sat on the sofa. He looked at the TV, the laptop, the phone. The noose.

He heard a car horn, saw the Dalmatian crossing the street.

In the following days, he put an ad in the paper. No one called. He repaired and secured the fence with bungee cords. Then with baling wire. Then with more chainlink. They didn't work. He used barbed wire. She dug a different hole under the fence.

He met neighbors he didn't know. Everyone wanted to pet the Dalmatian. They laughed at the dog's name, though it confirmed their suspicions of Carmichael. Some told him he better have the dog spayed.

Children laughed and screamed, running up to Disco. They couldn't believe Dalmatians were real. They wanted one!

You'll get plenty of chances to play with this one, their parents said.

Every day when he returned from work, he had to find the dog. He unknotted the noose, tied the dog to the back porch. When he came home, Disco was dragging half of a wooden porch support around the back yard.

He tried the mimosa tree. He found her stuck in the middle of the yard, chain wrapped around the trunk so that she couldn't move. The neighbor who had complained the most about the dog getting out told Carmichael it was a terrible thing to make a dog suffer. She threatened to call the cops.

He took her for a walk. She dragged him down the

sidewalk, smelling everything. They might as well run, he thought.

She could run longer and faster than Carmichael. They ran every day. Carmichael quit talking on the phone. The laptop stayed closed. He turned on the television but didn't change channels so much.

He bought a longer leash. His pace improved. He tugged her neck and barked her name every time she saw a squirrel she wanted to chase.

One day, he dropped the leash. This had happened before, but this time Carmichael didn't pick it up. Rounding a corner, they saw a black poodle in the yard. It barked. "Disco," Carmichael said.

She stayed beside him, without the tug from the leash, as long as they were running.

At home, he tried to teach her tricks. But the only one she learned she already knew: wagging her tail, nuzzling his hand to be petted.

"You would have never made it on *101 Dalmatians*," he told her. "Do you know that?"

She wagged her tail.

"You would never make it on TV."

She nodded, tried to get him to pet her.

"What kind of animal wants so much attention from one not its kind?" he asked.

She didn't answer. He saw his reflection in the blank TV screen.

"OK," he said, laughing. "Your turn. Give me a command. Teach me a trick."

She jumped onto the sofa beside him. Curled up, took a deep breath, and went to sleep.

Carmichael obeyed.

Odell Among Them

Shadowed by black oak and box elder, Odell looked down on the lighted throng and recalled the time when he too hoped heaven might be real.

Starting down the hill, his boot slid on a spray of acorns, and he fell, landing on the hand that held the gun. He wondered if God might be playing another game, then as quickly, cursed his foolishness. In his moment of truth Odell was becoming as weak as the holy rollers he was set to confront. He tucked the revolver in his boot and continued his descent.

***

The beatings began when Odell was nine. Falsehood and idleness were punished by lashes from a willow branch, which his father made him cut from the tree to enforce the notion that he brought the punishment on himself. When he turned 12, the instrument became a leather belt. The list of transgressions expanded to include questions about church beliefs and objections to interpretations of doctrine.

Thurman Odell, a deacon in the Church of Christ, owned a grocery store in the small town of Atoka. Odell deduced that the work did not please his father. Bored, the old man flirted with female customers, passed jokes he did not want church members to hear. They lived on a farm but, in spite of the church's advocacy of work, did not fulfill its potential for crops or livestock.

Thurman told his son, before one lashing, that he bestowed him with the name Ezekiel because it meant "God will strengthen." Odell replied with a question: "What name means God will confuse and deceive?"

He could not stand when the thrashing was concluded. He lay in the barn for hours, long enough to discover a stock of gas cans tucked in one corner behind the hay, draped by a moldy tarp. Odell thought it stupid to keep gas among the hay, then discovered the cans contained water, except one. This liquid was clear but it would not put out a fire.

Odell was 14 when he changed the contents of that can. He hugged his mother and sisters beforehand, women who distracted themselves with singing and gossip, crochet and dreams.

The boy would not have been punished for disposing of moonshine. Thurman, wary of detection, wouldn't have mentioned it. But when Odell asked his father how he liked getting drunk on gasoline, the worst beating of his life commenced. He took it, unable to silence his moaning. When it was done, he stood, still bleeding, fetched the knapsack he had stocked with clothes and canned food, and walked into the woods. He had run away before, only to be brought home by neighbors, church-goers who wouldn't believe a deacon would use the rod unless it was required. This time, Odell never returned.

***

Odell had seen a calf with five legs and a snake with two heads. He had witnessed a family of albinos and a boy with six fingers. But none of these things was as astonishing to him as the size of Farrel Graves' revival tent and the number of people who came to hear him speak.

Graves had been born in this county. The story in the paper allowed that in 1935 he was diagnosed with TB. Riding to the hospital in his parents' car, the Lord spoke to him. Whispering or a shout, the story didn't say. Yet the Lord offered to heal Graves if he would devote his life to God's service.

The theme of the revival was coming home to be made whole. Odell wondered how people, including his daughter, could think of a staked stretch of canvas as home. Some sap had allowed Graves use of his pasture for the tent, while another had done the same for the parking. Odell couldn't gauge who had suffered the worse deal. He guessed the car lot, but he might have been underestimating the damage done by the testimonial stomping of a thousand people. Two thousand shoes.

No one had factored the dust raised by so many automobiles on dirt section roads. Or if they had, there wasn't anything any of them, including Farrel Graves, could do about it. The county needed rain, and the roads and pastures were quick to release dust as a sign. Women wearing headscarves cupped their eyes with gloved hands. The men tugged fedoras and cowboy hats low, glad to have a handkerchief in their back pockets.

The paper proclaimed that Graves had established a worldwide following, holding tent revivals across the nation and in other countries, including Mexico and Australia. The meetings averaged eight thousand people. One had witnessed a record appearance of twelve thousand souls. There was talk of a televised show.

That figure was close to the total population of Girt County, and Graves admitted that while he didn't expect to set an attendance record at this revival, he had received word from God that something special was in store.

Odell chuckled at the thought of being an unexpected angel from the Lord, delivering a message of another kind.

***

Odell did little but work and eat. It was a time that would later be called the days when the men were made of iron and the derricks of wood. This was 1934. Sharecroppers were being blown off the land, but outside Seminole oil gushed so that men joked you should watch where you set your shovel.

There were many ignorant people, as many more mishaps. The wildcatters were still wild, but the oil had brought traders and families, and towns had been built. They were orderly and quiet. Odell could understand that. But a man who was different was not welcome. Odell couldn't understand that.

Raised in the church, he did not find comfort in the company of drink or cards. When he got lonely, he sat through a worship service. He ended up surveying an array of Christian styles. But the same people who glad-handed him at church wouldn't wave to him when he refused their invitation to return. They welcomed his questions but said, each in their own way, that only the Devil would abide more than one answer.

At age 20, he sat in the Beacon Café in Seminole, devouring eggs and coffee, sapped from 36 hours of work on a rig, fishing for a broken drill bit adrift in the hole. He was in no mood to listen to a loud voice tell someone else what to do, so when a fat patron talked nonsense babble to the young Indian girl who was cleaning the adjacent table, asking for a rain dance, Odell objected.

After he was done and the man lay bleeding on the floor, his buddies cowering in the booth, holding their hands as if he had drawn a gun, the owner added the cost of some broken plates to Odell's check in addition to a twenty-dollar fee for the disturbance or he would call the police and see him charged with assault. He chastised Odell for attacking a Christian man over a heathen.

Odell didn't speak, swallowing his desire to stomp the owner. When the man lit into the woman, who was named Lorraine, blaming her for the fight, Odell effectively persuaded him to shut up, claiming if he called the police he'd have to do so again, once Odell got out of jail, from a room in the Mission Hill Hospital.

Halfway out the door, Odell turned back to Lorraine, considering her plight, stuck at the café with an owner who was going to take his anger out on her. He told her to come on, he'd help her find work, and the men chortled until Odell stepped toward them.

Lorraine dropped her apron. On the sidewalk she told Odell she had never done that kind of work and Odell, blushing, said that wasn't what he meant. Lorraine said not for money anyway.

Odell had never heard a woman speak this way, at least not one who had a brain. He lived in a garage apartment, let to him by a Baptist preacher, so they drove out of town until they found a tree-shaded oil lease road. That night, Odell snuck her up to his room. She was a woman of cheekbones broad and smooth as river stones. Odell was a virgin. He had feared a confession, but with Lorraine, honesty was as natural as breath. Her hands on his skin were more refreshing than spring water, more uplifting than song.

She was a woman of few words, but she conveyed her past, and he to her. She was a child when her parents died, from diabetes and TB. She ended up at the Sisters of Mercy Catholic School where she was forbidden use of the Chickasaw language, spoken or signaled, or to learn the history of the tribe. She objected, called the headmaster Custer, the nuns blaggards, cursing them in Chickasaw. Her peers did not side with her because they believed the whites were going to give them houses and husbands and cars once they mastered the white ways.

The next day, Odell sought a new residence, unwilling to spend another day hiding from Christians.

They were evicted from two apartments for cohabitation. They spent a week camping, another in an abandoned barn. Unable to wed in Oklahoma, which wouldn't sanction interracial marriage, they drove to Kansas and found an obliging judge.

They worked, saved money, planned for a place in the country away from the intrusive Christians who would not speak to them except to tell them they were wrong and should be shunned.

***

Odell's anger solidified, as if his guts were fingers balling into a fist, during his sojourn down the hill. He had lost so much weight in the last year even his ankles had shrunk. The prospect of food made his bones grind.

The .38 shifted against his boot and ankle according to the turns of his foot. Darkness was slithering among the earth like a dream, overtaking the dust by the time Odell reached the congregation. He stopped at the side of the tent, gazing in amazement at the size of the canvas stretched toward the peak at the supporting poles. He wondered if Graves bought it used from a circus.

Odell had never taken his children to a circus. Sorrow swelled in him, pushing bile up his esophagus. He toed a stubborn clump of milkweed, coughed and spat. He would call this the day the Odells went to the big top.

The tent had rolled side flaps which ran the length of the thing. They had been released and staked. All Odell could see was the wedge of yellow light at the bottom and the left shoes of the people sitting nearest the side. And some black silhouettes within, clapping and romping and singing to the amplified music, which trumped the hum of the gas-powered generators in back of the tent and produced sounds that were as appetizing to Odell as a mouthful of soap.

He bent to withdraw the gun so he could position it beneath his belt but he saw a uniformed policeman step away from the lighted entrance to greet a tardy bunch of Christians walking up from the road. They exchanged greetings and dumb chuckles. The cop asked if he could search them for weapons. A woman gasped in protest while another said she had a Tommy gun in her purse. The officer laughed with them, and, tilting back his hat, said apologetically, "Not the ladies." For the men, he needed to peer inside their coats or check their pockets.

"Man in North Carolina fired at Mr. Graves. Said he felt the bullet whiz past his temple," one man observed.

"Won't happen here," a woman said, her white shoes coated in dust the color of her hose. "We're not crazy like those southerners."

"Nevertheless."

"I'd bet an angel changed the direction of that bullet with his wings," another man said. "But, of course, I don't bet."

Odell's handgun remained inside his right boot as he stepped into the light. He had tucked his jeans legs erratically into the boots and cocked his hat to better look like a hayseed. The line of cops and highway patrolmen tightened Odell's breathing.

"Where'd you come from fella?" an officer inquired.

"New Mexico," Odell said, tilting his sweat-stained straw hat back in the manner of the previous cop. "Least that's where I had to park."

The man chuckled and so did two highway patrolmen.

"Why didn't you across the road?"

"Man told me the lot was full."

"Can believe it. Where'd you park?"

"The road. Other side of that hill. Didn't want no one coming over the hill this side to hit me so I pulled plumb into the ditch."

"Be all right. Dry as it's been. Why didn't you walk down the road?"

"Well, I had to commit a crime. Hope you can forgive me. Maybe I'll ask Brother Graves to say—"

"What's that?"

Leaning closer, Odell said, "Drank too much coffee with supper. Had to relieve myself in the woods."

The man clapped Odell's shoulder. "Good luck finding a seat."

"Family's here. Should be saving one for me."

"They're getting righteous," the cop whispered. "But they ain't of a mind to allow an open seat."

***

They had two children. Lorraine named the girl, red and freckled like her father, Sunflower. Odell, who dropped the use of his Christian name, tagged the boy, dark and athletic like his mother, Rowdy.

The parents did not instruct their children in the ways of God or Jesus. There was no Bible in the home. They rented a lean-to farmhouse and spent their time outdoors, shooting rabbits and squirrels, growing tomatoes and corn, watching mockingbirds ward off an arrogant crow. Neither Odell nor the girl learned Lorraine's language, but the boy absorbed it along with his mother's view that the natural world was infused with spirit.

"The church-goers are right," she told the kids after dinner, placing a lightning-smoked sycamore log in the iron stove. "There is a soul. But they are blind to it in other things."

"Why?" Rowdy asked.

"Maybe they're afraid it will take theirs away."

"I can see why," Sunnie said. She had already asked the family to quit calling her Sunflower. "What would a coyote do with a soul? He just wants to eat."

"No, that's your father," Lorraine said.

"That's why I'm putting on weight," Odell said, finishing a slice of pecan pie. "I got saddled with a fat soul."

The children laughed but Lorraine just smiled and said, "Mm-hmm."

"You shouldn't speak about what you don't know about," Odell continued. "And if you can only be good to someone for the promise of reward, then..."

"What, wise father?" Lorraine asked.

"I don't know. Just don't do it."

"But how do you know there's not a God?" Sunnie asked.

"I don't know. But I haven't seen Him. If someone walks up who can feed us without me working, I'll follow him. Make my back quit hurting. But until then."

"That's what the Chickasaws meant by forked tongue," Lorraine said.

"What, a hurt back?"

"No, smart ass. Pointing to a God you can only know through them. Like a snake guarding its eggs."

"You're pretty smart for a squaw woman."

She was sitting beside Odell, his legs across her thighs. She reached under the leg of his tattered jeans, grabbed the skin and twisted until he cried, begging her to stop. "If invisible things don't exist, what is love then? Where is that?"

"Right here," Odell said, planting a kiss on Lorraine that

lasted long enough to make Rowdy not only grimace but command them to stop. Sunnie went to her room, closed the door.

The Odell children refused to identify their religious affiliations at school, and so were dubbed atheists or devil-worshippers, because of their Indian blood. Sunnie and Rowdy were often dismissed by other students, occasionally attacked. The boy learned to fight in the way of his father and earned back some respect. But the girl suffered, secretly telling friends she wanted to believe but didn't know how.

***

There were two sections of folding chairs, separated by a middle aisle marked by a succession of center posts. Two adjacent strings of yellow bulbs hung atop the aisle, with two other strips on the sides. A long row of lights hung above the portable stage whereon a man and a woman dressed in a pale blue suit and a white dress sang into microphones, accompanied by a band of guitars, piano, a drum, and a standing bass. Stacks of large speakers flanked the stage producing an amplification the likes of which Odell had never heard.

Many people were standing and clapping. Some would step into the aisle, which was overseen by suited ushers, and dance, testify, or talk in tongues. One man went with tonguing so long another took him up in the competition.

Odell stood, baffled. The Esteps, including Sunnie, were among this throng, but he couldn't spot them.

The music didn't stop. Occasionally, a man with greased hair took the microphone and exhorted the crowd to louder praise and greater heights of love for Jesus. A fat bastard worked himself to a froth with his upward-gazing and high-stepping. Sweat stains the width of pecan limbs spoiled his white shirt. When he landed a fat hand on Odell's shoulder, Odell was going to throw him to the ground until he saw the color rise in his broad bulb of a face. Then Jesus bid the man to fall.

Odell had to handle him like a heifer, spread legs and bent knees. Men were creating new lines of chairs brought in from a local church. Kicking two together, Odell plopped the man down. He contacted an usher just as the man pitched forward, facedown in the dust.

Aided by two cops and two other men, the man was stood then carted to a pickup which had delivered some of the folding chairs. As the truck pulled away for the hospital, Odell didn't have to ask why they didn't take the ailing man to Farrel Graves.

When the great healer was finally brought into view, he was accompanied by a musical red carpet befitting a State Fair headliner.

The man didn't look deformed yet his head bloomed from the stalk of his body like a pumpkin. His dark hair, slicked back and combed, formed a shallow V on his skull and rose from the pane of his forehead, disguising the size of his wide ears. Wearing a three-button suit and a matching brown tie, he paced the stage while the musicians played, raising a hand and mumbling, "Hallelujah."

He allowed the anticipation to build, slowing the music while he delivered in a low bass tone a streamed utterance that Odell initially mistook for tonguing but recognized as a demonstration of the man's speaking facility—a rapid yet precise monologue designed to show his greater skill to the aisle mumblers. He acted as if he had been in secret counsel with God before ascending the stage and was now offering an interpretation of the Lord's reassurance for His people. Apparently, Jesus and the Holy Ghost were in session with Graves and God as well.

The bandleader knew to follow Graves' rising tones, matching his pitch a count behind. By the time the crescendo was attained, the audience was bouncing and calling in heavenly passion.

This was not the form of worship Odell had been raised in,

but it seemed equally ludicrous to him. The solemn, high-minded piety of the Church of Christ had here been replaced by an exuberant desperation. None of it squared with the lessons Odell learned from his time among plants and animals.

Graves allowed the energy to ebb and the crowd to reseat before he addressed them with, "What do we want?"

The hopeful weren't afraid to respond.

Graves let the minions call, then quieted them with a still hand. "To come home," he offered, almost a whisper. "To return to that from which we came. Moses wandered. Abraham and Isaac. Elijah, Isaiah, Joseph, and Daniel. Saul of Tarsus, who left a false man and came home true." Graves waited for the applause of amens. "And Jesus. Our Savior. God's only son. The Lord Jesus Christ. The only whole man. He wandered. And he came home."

The response was charged. "I have come home, as Jesus, as the prophets, but like them, not to stay. I am proud of this county, proud of its people and its hills, proud of its lush bounty and its thorny groves. But I cannot stay at this home. Jesus could not remain in Nazareth and you will not find sanctuary in the quilted bed where you lay your tired body tonight. No. There is only one home for Christians. For me. For Jesus. And for you. And that's why I have come to the place of my birth. To make you whole. To remove the blight and fill your heart with the spirit so you may be prepared for your true home with God."

Graves gestured and the man with black hair brought forth a folding chair identical to those that sat the audience. The man placed a decorative pillow, stitched by an old Christian woman, on the seat. Graves regarded the gift, mumbled a prayer of thanks and a blessing on the woman's soul, and tossed it to the stage floor. "Their chairs aren't padded," he said, groaning as he sat.

On cue, all lights went out except for those directly above Graves. Settling, the man removed a white handkerchief from his pocket, wiped his sweaty forehead, and loosed his tie.

"To come home. Where we will be healed and made whole.

Where death cannot gain a foothold, nay even a glimpse."

He gazed at the floor as if he were reading the truth in a crystal pool. He didn't speak. He let the other Christians shout praise and support, stilling them without word or gesture. When he looked up, his expression suggested he was peering into a harsh light. He grimaced for the adults, yet held out his hand as if were speaking to gentle children.

"I have not returned home from my mission abroad to other countries and continents, from among the hostile Arabs and heathen Africans, the skeptical Europeans, and the crazy Australians, to recite scripture and verse for you, God-fearing people. Because you know the Bible. You know God's word. No. I have returned to testify to you about the miracles God wants to bring to you, to the power of healing that comes to the faithful heart and home. I would not be here before you if God had not heard my cry in the wilderness of Girt County and given me sight." The man's voice rose. "The Lord allowed me to heal the lame and the constricted and the diseased so I might show you the way. God has called this many souls to a revival in the woods because He and His love and His healing powers want to show you the way. He wants to make you whole and say to you those two words you want to hear: come home." Voices rose. Graves waited. Then, as if he were whispering in the ear of a dying man: "But your heart and your soul must be right to enter those gates. Do you hear me? Do you? Hear me?" After the roar, Graves said, "I have returned to the county of my birth to encourage some, to heal some, to scold some, to love all and to be your shepherd home!"

The man could weave words, Odell gave him that. Yet while the others appeared to be losing their burdens, Odell felt the weight of time in his neck and feet. And the gun in his boot.

***

When Rowdy turned twelve, the family purchased a rough acreage and began the construction of a home. The foundation was formed of anything that wouldn't rust or rot, at least for a decade. Unaccustomed to floor plans, Odell marked the width and length in a rectangle he thought appropriate for size and cost, then he and Rowdy raised the frame. Excepting the kitchen sink and single toilet and bath, he had Lorraine map the walls of the other rooms. She smiled with every step as if she'd won a thousand dollars.

While the men worked on the home, the women picked up pecans from the abundant trees, which were so plentiful that year the Odells took to piling the unshelled nuts behind the house instead of buying more baskets.

They ran short of money and had to roof the house with tin they scavenged from neglected barns. The kids loved the clamor of hard rain on the roof. They could be loud as they wanted.

Odell plowed the ground with a battered tractor, built fence with bois d'arc posts, teaching Rowdy to use the come-along as they stretched the wire. He started a herd. For Christmas, he brought home a dappled pony. That night, Lorraine made him feel twenty years old.

But the following April, Rowdy came home from school then snuck off from his chores, riding the horse across the back of the property. He crossed the creek and rode over a hill, guiding the pony at a walk past cedar and black oak. The woods grew dense and he was set to turn back when he came upon a small pond in a neglected clearing. Impervious to the cool wind whipping up from the south, Rowdy was mesmerized by a flock of red-wing blackbirds perched in the cattails, chattering like school kids. He kicked off his boots, rolled his jeans, and crept among them without flushing the birds. Impressed by his stealth, he wondered if he could go native, in the old ways of his mother's stories, and catch a fish with his hands. In time, he spied perch swimming near his bare legs, biting his hairs, but he couldn't snag one. He left the water and with his pocket knife carved a sharp point on a sumac branch. He hoped to spear a fish. He never noticed the bruised, ominous thunderhead that rolled in, carrying javelins of lightning.

The family waited until dusk before Odell went searching, but the storm drove him back to the house. After midnight, rain still falling but the wind and lightning abated, Odell set out again. When he found the pony, sequestered beneath a mulberry tree, he stopped, dumb as the horse.

He found Rowdy at dawn, face down in the water, hair floating like moss. He couldn't detect a wound until he had carried the boy back to the house. By the way his head lolled Odell deduced his neck had snapped. Maybe thunder had spooked the horse, which had thrown its rider. Odell recited his observations to the sobbing women, but he didn't cry. Reaching his assessment, he waited for Rowdy to rise. He prepared a quilt pallet on the hardwood floor and set about to repair his son.

Odell spoke to him, lay hands on him. Lorraine went for a doctor. The next day she brought an old medicine woman. Odell would not accept their diagnoses. He rubbed the boy's chest for hours. Finally, he resorted to prayer, weeping from fear at the thought of God striking down infidels who defied Him with rods from the sky, begging the Lord to take him instead.

On the third day, Odell left the body for a half hour, insisting Rowdy not be touched. They did not possess a phone, so Odell drove into town. He obtained change he carried curled in the tail of his shirt, and with the aid of a sympathetic operator, located the number of Farrel Graves' congregation in Piedmont, where Graves had started his church and launched his campaign.

Yes, the assistant pastor replied, Pastor Graves had performed many miracles, through God, of course. And, yes, he whispered, Pastor Graves had raised a man from the dead on a campaign through Tennessee.

Odell described his son's plight, gave the man directions to his home, promising any amount of money or labor in return, offering his home and property, a lifetime of service from a man and woman who could work eighteen-hour days. The man sympathized. He would gladly deliver the message.

He wanted Odell to know that supporting Pastor Graves' crusade would make Odell's soul shine in God's eyes like an angel's wings. Odell repeated the directions, provided the phone number of a neighbor. The man seemed to take the information, but he reiterated that God healed, not Pastor Graves, who was His servant, His Holy Conduit.

"Tell him to transfer it to me," Odell said. "Or the doctor. We'll give it right back."

The man praised the Lord and hung up.

Rowdy remained in the home two more days. It took six men to remove him, two to carry the body, four to restrain his father.

It was assumed a preacher would perform the service. The funeral parlor made the arrangements. Odell didn't object until the man, a Free Will Baptist, spoke on the demands of salvation, rather than of the boy he didn't know. Odell took the podium from the man but he couldn't speak of Rowdy either. He launched a tirade against God. Several men, including a deputy asked to attend because of Odell's reputation, stepped forward but Odell let go the sermon, asked that they get on with it. One of the men went after Sunnie, who fled the parlor in response to her father.

Only Lorraine was able to cope with the loss. She worked outside during the day, taking long walks in the woods; at night, she held herself, rocked and moaned, conjuring Rowdy's spirit in her dreams. Odell no longer winced when he banged a finger with a hammer. He couldn't taste fruit. Sugar made him vomit. When Lorraine attempted to hold him in bed, he threw her off.

Sunnie wouldn't speak. She was often late coming home from school and made requests to spend the night with friends many Saturday nights, returning after dark on Sunday evening. Lorraine knew the girl was finding solace in a place the family didn't go, but Odell was too preoccupied to ask.

On her sixteenth birthday she attended a quiet celebration with her parents and one friend. The next day she didn't come home from school. She called that evening. She was moving out. She didn't identify her location.

Odell didn't bother with the sheriff. By week's end he found her, sequestered with the Esteps, a clan of Pentecostals. They lived in the country, tending goats and vegetables. The men earned a living hauling salt water from oil wells to storage tanks. The women didn't cut their hair, wear pants or make-up. They made bread and played piano in frame homes that housed no televisions.

Odell confronted them with a shotgun and was met with the same in return. They were at least pretending to act as men, and had been smart enough to fan across the face of the house instead of grouping on the porch where Odell could've picked two off with a single shot.

The sight of an Estep with his hat and shoes and Bible and stupid grin cinched Odell's scrotum. They didn't take to the sun. They were always in the shade of a hat or porch or church. Their skins were pale as meringue. Odell hated meringue.

The grandfather informed him he was trespassing and held no claim. Sunnie had married his grandson in a church ceremony two nights before.

Odell didn't speak, astounded. He shifted his target from one man to the other. He saw their concentration relax and wondered if he might not be able to take them, blasting one then jumping behind the pickup door, which he'd left open.

"You should know she's come of her own accord," the elder Estep announced.

"She didn't drive herself."

"We can take her back. Allow her to do the driving. She's sixteen."

"Too young to make this decision."

"The soul is never too young to be called to the Lord. You're old enough to know that." The Esteps chuckled at the old man's wit. Odell felt the weight of the weapon in his hands. "We had a young man led a revival wasn't but fourteen."

"'Bout the age ya'll are acting." Odell had to laugh at his own retort.

"Why don't you put that gun and your hatred down and let's talk about where the source of your anger might lie."

"I'm staring at it."

"What have you to lose? Except the soul you claim doesn't exist."

"The truth. That's what I got to lose. That's what Sunnie…"

"I am the way and the truth and the life, Jesus said. No man comes to the Father but by me." The groom amened.

"I have hair, two legs, and can roar. That don't make me a goddamn bear."

"A man can spend all his days in jest. That doesn't mean he'll be laughing come judgment day."

"And he won't be flying through the clouds with wings neither. Sunnie!" Odell bellowed. "Come out here and honor your family."

Sunnie poked her head out the front door, ashen. "Daddy, I've been called. I know you don't understand. Neither does Mama. But she knows love when she sees it. She's not blind with hate like you."

"I don't hate. I—"

"Jesus is love. He has opened my heart. I'm not picking another family over ours. I'm spreading—"

"Then marry Jesus. Not this Estep."

"I'm marrying both."

The Esteps praised this reply.

"You're still in shock over Rowdy."

"No, you are. I'm doing something about it. Before it's too late."

The clan cheered and clapped.

"You better start repenting," the groom proclaimed, taking Sunnie in his arms. He had to be twenty-two but still couldn't grow the hint of a beard. "That kind of blasphemy, you'll need the rest of your days to receive God's forgiveness."

"Now, son," the old man said. "See how anger can corrupt. Remember Saul of Tarsus. God could turn this man's soul in a heartbeat. If only he would allow it. Maybe you'll come to hear

God's prophet Farrel Graves next week. Holding a revival."

"Farrel Graves?" Odell called. "You're renouncing your father and mother for him?"

Shaking her head, Sunnie started to explain but no one heard her because Odell raised his weapon as if Graves had become a target mounted on the porch. The Esteps responded, aiming and shaking. Odell was ready to deliver a couple of them to their maker but recognized that he wouldn't get out alive, leaving his daughter to deal with the Esteps alone, and Farrel Graves, the charlatan, to have the last laugh.

***

He thought of the length of the sermon he was about to endure, the invitation following. He didn't care to wait that long. He scanned the aligned heads for a glimpse of his daughter. He didn't find her.

Odell knew what he had to do but his plan required its own leap of faith and Odell didn't readily release possession of anything, including himself. But by the time he was five rows down the aisle, he felt as if he'd leapt out of himself. His intentions were working his body, which trailed behind like a stringed puppet.

He walked straight-legged, swinging both arms and legs, as if he'd been wound up with panic and struck with rigor mortis at the same moment. He reasoned that a normal walk toward the stage would attract the ushers' attention much quicker than a deranged act.

Ushers, positioned in aisle seats every ten rows, stood to intercept Odell once he drew near Graves. He rushed past the first men, uttering nonsense. When he became outnumbered, he cried out, "I'm dying. Someone help me, I'm dying. I ain't lying!"

He careened, whopping ushers in the jaw with his flailing arms. Once they stopped his progress and pinned his arms, twelve rows from the stage, Odell raised his plaintive voice, pleading for help.

Graves instructed them to release the ailing man. Two ushers resisted his instruction, shaking their heads, but Graves commanded them. No one under the tent made a sound as Odell straight-legged his way to the stage. He stopped at the feet of the great healer, who had not stood, preferring to stare down at Odell from his lighted throne.

Odell looked at the man's nose, his large nostrils, the cluster of hairs within, the acorned blotch beside his forehead, wanting to ask him why God would speak to him and not to other men. Instead, Odell shouted, "I'm ailing!" Then, in a flash of weakness, he added, "Don't want no one to die! My son—"

Farrel Graves extended a hand to grant a healing touch to Odell's head and pray for him. That was Odell's cue. He steeled himself, angered by the man's pretense of power over the natural world. Odell didn't intend to kill the man. He planned to shame him. Playing the fool, Odell would ask Graves to demonstrate his miraculous abilities: heal himself from a gunshot. He knew Graves would play him off, and he would have to turn mean and insistent. He would demand Graves perform the miracle or admit he held no authority. Odell figured Graves would create an explanation after all was said and done, but those with eyes would see the charlatan for what he was. He could only hope his daughter hadn't been completely blinded.

On contact with Graves' hand, Odell dropped. He went to ground rather than the waiting arms of an attendant. The crowd gasped. Ushers closed in.

Odell intended to use the move as a distraction so he could retrieve his revolver, but he snapped his head on the hard, dry dirt, jolting his brain pan and senses.

He awakened new to the world, though no time had passed. He had to blink his memory and intentions back. The fall had shaken his anger but when he saw the ushers crowding in, he twitched, thrashing the ground, calling out nonsense, aware as he did that he was no good at tonguing.

Opening his eyes, still on the ground, he reached for the

gun. Beside his boot he saw a pair of veiled legs. Tracing them, he met a plain cotton dress and blue blouse with a floral pattern. Flame-orange hair, the color of his as a boy, gained his attention next.

"I knew you would be touched," Sunnie said, tears streaming her face. "It's a miracle. They do happen. Pastor Graves is right. I knew if I had faith in prayer and courage of convictions." She wiped her cheeks with her palms as she reached down to help her father to his feet. "We'll see Rowdy in heaven now. We'll all be together and healed."

She was aided in her effort by the Esteps, but when Odell reached his feet, she hugged his chest and would not let go. He felt her sorrow and her hope stream into him. And her love. The invisible things.

"The Lord has seen and recognized us tonight," Graves proclaimed. "I healed our first sinner and just barely touched him."

The audience cheered. Those who didn't hear asked their neighbor to repeat what the pastor had said. The ushers motioned for the Esteps to return to their row of chairs. Odell walked with them but they all stopped in response to Graves. The man was stone serious as he rose. "I feel a great wound here," he said, staring at Odell, pointing. "A soul struggling against the grip of Satan's despair. Let us pray for this man who has had the courage to show us the way home."

Everyone bowed their heads but Odell as Graves prayed. Many closed their eyes, some murmured along. Odell was embarrassed at first from the attention, but noting the scores of bent heads, mouths offering thanks and concern on his behalf, he became touched by the sincerity of the response.

He would not let go of his daughter's hand but he removed his hat, lowered his head out of respect. When he did, he noticed the visible handle of his gun hung on the lip of his boot. He turned to Graves. The gun fell within the man's line of vision, but the pastor's eyes remained closed while he prayed. Odell wondered what the man had seen, what vision had prompted his blessing. But in the same breath Odell let it go. It was his nature to question. It was Graves' to pray.

***

That night, in bed, he made Lorraine uncomfortable by regarding her face, stroking her cheeks and cracked lips. Maybe she was right. Maybe there was spirit in her yellowed teeth, soul in the patch of gray hair above her temple, as real as death and decay. He would never know in this world. When he traced the bridge of her nose then her hairline with his rough thumb, she smiled in embarrassment. Her bottom lip on one side drew back lower than the other, just as Rowdy's did when he grinned.

"Ge-tsi-ka-hv-da a-ne-gv-i," she muttered.

"What's that?"

"The trail where they cried."

And Odell did. Her words found the well within him. But the seams beside his eyes looked like the webbing of a cradle as he and Lorraine completed a holy embrace.

About the Author

Mark Walling has published stories, poems, and essays in numerous literary magazines and anthologies. He teaches creative writing at East Central University in Ada, Oklahoma. This is his first book.

Acknowledgments

Several stories in this collection first appeared in the following publications:

Del Sol Review, "The Year I Lost My Ass"
Sewanee Review, "Bois d'Arc"
South Dakota Review, "Bear's Brother"
RE:AL, "Mama's Boy"
Blood & Aphorisms, "A Coke and a Cigarette"
Hobart, "One Dalmatian"
Concho River Review, "Odell Among Them"

Special thanks to Paul Bowers.

Milton Keynes UK
Ingram Content Group UK Ltd.
UKHW010944221123
433051UK00009B/499

9 798986 899411